NOT NOW

(A Camille Grace FBI Suspense Thriller—Book 2)

Kate Bold

Kate Bold

Bestselling author Kate Bold is author of the ALEXA CHASE SUSPENSE THRILLER series, comprising six books (and counting); the ASHLEY HOPE SUSPENSE THRILLER series, comprising six books (and counting); the CAMILLE GRACE FBI SUSPENSE THRILLER series, comprising five books (and counting); and the HARLEY COLE FBI SUSPENSE THRILLER series, comprising three books (and counting).

An avid reader and lifelong fan of the mystery and thriller genres, Kate loves to hear from you, so please feel free to visit www.kateboldauthor.com to learn more and stay in touch.

ISBN: 978-1-0943-9483-1

BOOKS BY KATE BOLD

ALEXA CHASE SUSPENSE THRILLER
THE KILLING GAME (Book #1)
THE KILLING TIDE (Book #2)
THE KILLING HOUR (Book #3)
THE KILLING POINT (Book #4)
THE KILLING FOG (Book #5)
THE KILLING PLACE (Book #6)

ASHLEY HOPE SUSPENSE THRILLER
LET ME GO (Book #1)
LET ME OUT (Book #2)
LET ME LIVE (Book #3)
LET ME BREATHE (Book #4)
LET ME FORGET (Book #5)
LET ME ESCAPE (Book #6)

CAMILLE GRACE FBI SUSPENSE THRILLER
NOT ME (Book #1)
NOT NOW (Book #2)
NOT WELL (Book #3)
NOT HER (Book #4)
NOT NORMAL (Book #5)

HARLEY COLE FBI SUSPENSE THRILLER
NOWHERE SAFE (Book #1)
NOWHERE LEFT (Book #2)
NOWHERE TO RUN (Book #3)

PROLOGUE

The boys were unaware of how quiet the forest had gone in their presence. All they cared about was enjoying the day. School started next week, after all, and they wanted to milk every bit of fun they could from these last few days.

PJ led the duo through the forest as they quickly approached the mucky grounds of the swamp. Donald, or just "Donnie," ran a bit behind him, raising a hand to swat away the branches that came sailing back at his face as PJ passed by.

"Not so fast!" Donnie said. "Keep it up and your ass will end up in the swamp!"

He said the word "ass" louder than the rest. They were ten years old and words like that could only be spoken out here in these familiar woods, away from parents and teachers.

"That's the point!" PJ responded.

They'd been out here thousands of times. When they were younger, they played ninja out here, battling with sticks as swords. Things were a bit more mature now, though. Now, it was all about seeing who could do the dumbest thing of all. And today's dumb thing was dipping a foot or maybe even a whole leg into the swamp waters.

They'd never been out quite this far, as the swamp loomed ahead somewhere. Of course, they'd heard all the warnings about the dangers that lurked deep in these woods, especially once you reached the swamp. Leeches. Snakes. Gators.

Jimmy Elridge, a kid from their rec-league soccer team, swore he'd seen a python out here one time.

But as a ten-year-old boy, wasn't the danger part of the fun?

Suddenly, PJ came to a stop. He stopped so abruptly that Donnie almost ran directly into his back.

"What is it?" Donnie asked.

"We're there. Look...right there. And you were right. I did almost fall into it."

The boys looked out to the swamp and Donnie was already thinking of the tales of bravery and exploration they'd be able to tell on their first day back at Hen Creek Elementary. He studied the swamp closely, wanting to make sure he got every detail right. It looked like a pure sheet of mud at the start, and then it became something more. It looked like what Donnie imagined a broken sewage line might spill out. It looked dark, like the stuff of legends where people were drowned in moats and eaten by large fish.

"I didn't think it would be this bad," Donnie said.

And this was just the edge of the swamp. The real danger lay ahead. The boys continued forward, stepping over cypress trees that had fallen to the ground, long ago victims of a hurricane. The fallen trees made a slow-moving river in the forest, a river that led straight to the swamp and into the muck.

The boys approached the edge of the swamp, to a place where a fallen log met the edge of the mud. The log lay on its side and this was the edge of the safe area. Once they stepped off the log, they'd be in the deep waters of the swamp.

"It looks pretty gross in there!" PJ said.

Donnie looked down into the murky waters. The muck was too deep for him to see a thing.

"You first?" PJ asked.

"Sure." Donnie hoped PJ couldn't tell just how scared he was. What had they been thinking? They didn't *have* to do this. They could still brag about it back at school.

"And be quick," PJ said. "I wanna get out of here before the snakes meet up with the gators and we get caught in the middle."

"Not funny."

Donnie's gaze roamed the sludge-green waters, the occasional lily pad and reed. Then, holding his breath and with his heart slamming in his chest, he dipped his toes in the water. He almost stopped to take off his flip flop, but it was too late. His foot was already going in.

His first thought was that the water was much warmer than he'd been expecting. Like, *much* warmer. There was also a lot of movement as tadpoles and God only knew what else went flitting against his ankle.

"Go to the knee!" PJ said, chuckling gleefully.

Donnie put more of his leg in. It really wasn't *that* bad. Hell, maybe he'd go in all the way to his waist. He'd have to explain the wet shorts to his mom, but he could—

His foot hit something. Something big and solid. Something that felt alive.

Donnie screamed and yanked his foot back. He moved so quickly that he tripped over the log behind them. PJ cackled with laughter, one hand clutching his laughing stomach and the other pointing at Donnie.

"You klutz! You should see yourself!"

"PJ, there's something in there! Get away. It might be a croc!"

"What? You serious?"

"Yes! Let's go, man!"

Donnie got to his feet and when he did, his eyes instantly went back to that murky water. He was sure there would be a croc or a python coming out of the water for them at any moment.

He *did* see something, but it was not a croc or a large snake.

It was something that seemed much less dangerous but *looked* a bit scarier.

It was a person.

A dead woman.

It bobbed to the surface of the water, having been disturbed by Donnie's foot. The skin was waxy and pale, the dead eyes nearly colorless, opened and looking up at the sky.

The boys shared one look, PJ nearly in tears, and then they ran.

Donnie let out a scream that tore through the forest, so horrified and panicked that those birds that had gone quiet in their presence took flight, the beats of their wings like little claps of thunder.

CHAPTER ONE

Camille Grace looked around her new office and smiled. It was a small office, located in the lower level of a branch of the FBI that tended to stay busy. Somehow, she'd ended up back in New Orleans, the shadow of her childhood just about an hour away. She'd been given this office with an apology, the HR department figuring she'd take it as something of an insult.

But as far as Camille was concerned, it was perfect. It was far away from everyone else, and it was quiet. Looking around and realizing she still had quite a bit of setting up to do, she looked back over the last few days and tried to make sense out of exactly how she'd arrived here.

When Camille left Alabama behind, she'd done it without any emotion. The worst of it had been leaving her boyfriend. Declan had put up a bit of a fight, but in the end Camille was pretty sure he'd been just as relieved as she was. She also thought the move brought on no emotion because there was some broken thing inside of her that had always known her path would lead her back to Louisiana.

Upping had been there, waiting for her like a bad habit she'd once dropped and was now returning to. There was a comfort to it, sure, but there was danger there as well. She was living in an apartment just outside of New Orleans, but Upping was less than an hour south and sometimes she could hear it calling.

She'd expected Director Milton at the FBI to throw some obstacles up when she'd requested the transfer, but he seemed okay with it. In fact, he'd acted like Camille had presented him with a gift. He'd hated to see her go, or so he said, but there were three current openings with the New Orleans field office, so it worked out great.

And just like that, just fifteen days after closing a case in New Orleans and briefly revisiting her place in Alabama, Special Agent Camille Grace was heading back to Louisiana. It was the place she'd been raised and the place where her entire life had been torn apart at the age of twelve.

The echoes of her previous life in Upping had hovered over her ever since she arrived. It's why she'd worked so hard to settle quickly into her new job. Somehow, she'd managed to acquire a small office in the basement of the field office. Never having had an office before, she took great pride in setting it up as she settled in.

Determined to make a good impression and get off on the right foot with her new partners, she'd even gone so far as to order a desk, a filing cabinet, and a small couch. Everything was a mess now, but soon it would be neat and tidy, totally unlike her.

She'd been a little surprised that the only one of her new coworkers she'd met so far was Assistant Director Marie McCutcheon. As the director's right hand, she was the one who brought Camille into the office. She'd been told that AD McCutcheon was the best thing to happen to the New Orleans field office in a long time. The woman was straight as an arrow and hard as a rock. Camille detested such analogies, but she'd quickly discovered that they were true. She was fifty but had the body of someone that hadn't hit forty yet. She carried herself with great confidence that was accentuated with the fact that she knew every man she passed did a double take. Yet somehow, she seemed to not let it go to her head.

The woman's absolute aura was why Camille had still not divulged everything about her past to McCutcheon. She didn't want to be seen as the new agent that dragged in a ton of baggage with her.

On her third full day in her office, which was nearly organized at that point, Camille found herself doing that same old balancing act again. She already liked McCutcheon quite a bit and she could tell the feeling was mutual, so she hated telling lies. So she did her best to simply omit information as McCutcheon once again brought up the fact that Camille had grown up just an hour to the south.

"You got much family out there in Upping?" McCutcheon asked.

"Some. A father and a woman that wasn't really an aunt but might as well have been."

"Ah, the unofficial aunt," McCutcheon said. "Those are the best kind. You been out to visit them at all?"

"Not yet. But I did see the not-aunt a few weeks back. I think she was actually one of the reasons it was so easy for me to decide to relocate."

"You all moved in to your apartment?"

Camille grinned and nodded. "Yeah. It's pretty easy when you don't have that much stuff."

McCutcheon shrugged. "Enjoy it. I have no regrets about my twenties, but I *can* tell you it's going to go by fast. Especially here. We've all heard great things about you, Grace. Even aside from the Sir

Richard bust. I'll make sure you stay busy. New Orleans and the surrounding areas, as I'm sure you know, is never going to disappoint."

"Yes, I know."

"Well, I'll leave you to your office set-up for now. Hopefully I'll have something worth your while sooner rather than later."

With McCutcheon gone, Camille sat on her new couch, a couch that took up nearly the entire back wall of her office. She thought of her "non-aunt" Deanna Lewiston. She wanted to go see her soon because she hadn't even told Deanna that she was living in New Orleans.

But she could do that later. She knew where she *had* to go. When she'd spoken to Deanna a little over two weeks ago, Deanna had told her the news about her father. He was sick and no one knew what he was sick with because the stubborn bastard wouldn't go to the doctor.

She'd come back here with such ease and it had felt...well, maybe not *right* but something akin to right. It had felt that way despite the fact that her father was still in Upping.

She had to go see him. It was the last thing she wanted to do. She could far too easily recall the horrors he'd caused, the way he'd tore their family apart. The way she'd been terrified of him for most of her life. There were scars from her childhood she'd not yet fully recovered from, and her father was at the base of them—scars that had also pushed her mother and sister away. Her father…the pig pen…the mystery around what had pushed him to certain actions.

But he was sick, and she was here.

Camille looked at her watch. Four-thirty.

"Later," she said. "Maybe I'll have some beer. Maybe that'll make it tolerable."

Speaking it out loud served as an odd form of accountability. And though there was nothing stopping her from leaving right then and there, Camille sat on the couch a bit longer. She wasn't worried about summoning up the courage to face him.

No, she was more worried about how she'd react to the mere sight of him.

So she sat on the couch and waited, once again feeling her hometown grumbling from a distance like a bad storm that was pushing in her direction.

***

The one godsend Camille got was that her father no longer lived in the house where she'd grown up. When he'd gotten out of prison several years ago, he'd moved into a small one-bedroom house at the back end of Upping. It was tucked into a half-circle of a clearing that was surrounded by gloomy-looking trees to all sides.

Like most of the houses and mobile homes on this stretch of rural Louisiana, the place was a rental. Camille knew all of this because she'd done some digging from her new office in the days leading up to the visit. So when she pulled her new-to-her car into her father's driveway at six o' clock on the same day she and McCutcheon had talked about the importance of "non-aunts," she was ready.

The six pack of beer would hopefully help as well.

She parked behind an old Ford pickup, the R worn off of the logo on the tailgate. She wasn't sure how to feel about the fact that she was not nervous when she stepped up to the porch and knocked on the door. If anything, it felt natural. Deep down, it felt like something she should have done a long time ago.

Yet when she heard footfalls and the sound of the door opening, there *was* a slight pang of nerves. But by then, it was too late. By then, her father was standing in the doorway, looking out at her.

Carl Grace had changed drastically and from one simple glance at him she could tell that Deanna had been right. He was sick.

He was a stout man, with a wide frame and a belly that had grown wide. His hair was gray and unkempt. His eyes were a bit watery and his skin was pale. It wasn't just the fact that his hair was a lot thinner than it had been the last time Camille had seen him.

It was the look in his eyes. They looked like the windows of a house that had been broken into. When Camille looked at her father, she saw every horrible thing he'd ever done to her or her mother, or anyone else for that matter, in his eyes. She saw the coldness there, the self-centeredness. She saw the latent rage and fire that had once resided there. Even if those things were no longer present, they'd done their damage.

Those eyes seemed to glisten as he studied her. Three seconds went by before he gathered what was happening.

"Camille?" he said, his voice a whisper.

"Yeah," she replied, surprised at how calm she sounded. "It's me...it's Camille."

"My God...my baby girl..." His voice was even weaker than before.

But what came as the biggest shock of all was that she didn't feel anything. No anger or fear or sadness or relief. Instead, his voice and that last comment brought to mind something else he'd said in the past.

My baby girl. Why'd you have to be so good? Haven't you heard of the slaughterhouse? Haven't you seen the dead hogs?

He said nothing else after this. He looked at her and then quickly back behind him. He looked sad, maybe a little embarrassed. She could only imagine what he was living like out here, sick and alone in the middle of nowhere.

"You don't have to invite me in," she said.

He looked put-off by this comment, but he nodded and stepped aside. "No, no, come on in. It's just...I've been by myself for a very long time now and..."

"No maid service," Camille said, trying to keep the mood light. "I get it."

She followed him into the living room. There was a couch, a tattered armchair and a TV sitting on top of an old entertainment center. Carl Grace sat across from her in the armchair and when Camille looked at him, she saw a tear rolling down his cheek.

"How're you doing, Dad?" she asked, trying to sound casual.

"I'm doing fine.

"Fine? You look like hell, Dad. Deanna says you're sick. And looking at you, I'd say she's right."

"You've talked to Deanna?"

"Yes."

"Why…what are you doing here? I mean, I'm *so* glad to see you, but you're the last person I'd expect to see in Upping."

"I'm on a case in New Orleans," she lied.

"And you wanted to come by to see me?"

"Not originally, no. I won't lie about that." Amazed at how easy it was to speak to him, she added: "But when I knew you were sick, I figured I should."

"She shouldn't have told you."

"Why not?"

He lowered his eyes. "Because I'm dying, Camille. I'm dying, and it's not a pretty sight. I'm in a lot of pain right now and I don't want you to see me like this."

"Well, it was either like this or not at all. And how do you know you're dying? How do you know if you won't go to the doctor?"

"I did go to the doctor. I just didn't tell Deanna. I got the results last week. It's pancreatic cancer and it's pretty far along."

"Jesus, Dad. What are you going to do? Just stay here and suffer with it?"

"That was the plan."

A silence fell in around them. Camille took the time to look around the place beyond the living room. A small kitchen was joined to the living room, connected by a bar area. The sink was filled with dirty dishes.

"You gonna let those get warm or were they a peace offering?"

She noticed he was nodding to the beer she'd brought in. A six pack of Coors bottles. She took one out and tossed it to him; he caught it and uncapped it right away, like a true professional.

"They aren't a peace offering," Camille said. "They were just something to do. Something to fill the silence."

He took a long pull from his and sighed. "You must think it's stupid, me not ever seeking treatment for it. Right?"

"I do."

"What else did Deanna tell you? Did she tell you about your mother?"

"That she died all alone in a hotel room in Texas? Yeah."

"And if you—"

"You know what, Dad?" she said. "It was a big enough step for me to come see you at all. I don't know if I'm ready for small talk. Especially not if you're about to tell me you've chosen to suffer through this because you deserve it. Because of all you did in the past."

He laughed, but it was a sad sound. "Damn, you're good. That's exactly what I'm doing you know?"

She nodded. She wasn't surprised at his admission of it, but she did find that she was upset about how he legitimately didn't seem to care. And, more to the point, how much she discovered she *did* care.

"Can we just sit for now? I don't think I need to talk. I think I'm going to drink two of these beers and leave the rest for you. And then I'm going to go."

She saw the glint of sadness in his eyes and didn't feel at all ashamed that it brought her a bit of joy. "So you just came to confirm that I was dying? And then...what? You're just going to go?"

"Yes," she said, enjoying the freedom of it. "For now. But I'll be in town for a while. You'll see me again." She almost asked if there was anything he needed but bit back. She wasn't quite there yet.

Instead, she sat in silence and rather enjoyed it. She sat in silence in the presence of a man that was both oddly familiar and eerily strange at the same time. She drank and took the occasional glance at the man that had raised her and yet, somehow, had made her childhood a nightmare.

More than that, though, being around her father reminded her of Nanette—of a sister that had been missing for far too long. And even if Nanette was dead, Camille needed to know. It was a stark reminder of why she was really here, why she'd felt such a need to come back. It was a reminder that she knew would haunt her like a deranged ghost until she finally got to the bottom of it.

A ghost that was already tickling the back of her neck, asking what the hell was taking her so long.

CHAPTER TWO

Deputy Rick Humphrey watched the little aluminum boat make its way through the stagnant, swampy waters ahead of him. The gnats were out in full force, swarming around his head in an annoying little cloud. He swatted at them with his hat, the widening bald spot at the back of his head cooled with the hat gone.

There were two men out in the boat: a local officer that knew these swamps just as well as anyone else in the area, and a local outdoor jock that worked just about any kind of boat like an instrument.

The jock's name was Ben something or other. He looked both irritated and excited. They'd called on him before, needing help in the swamps, so he was somewhat used to police business. But the business of dragging the water for bodies apparently didn't sit well with him.

They'd pulled a body out of the water yesterday. It had been a local woman, name of Wendy Pullman. Wendy had been discovered by two boys out for a stroll, which was good because Wendy had been missing for three days.

It was bad, though, because Wendy was the second body they'd found in a swampy area in the last four days. And like the first body, it appeared that Wendy had been attacked by a gator.

It hadn't been a pretty sight. Half of her left leg had been gnawed to the bone, a chunk had been taken out of her shoulder, and she'd been missing three fingers on her left hand. It was the grisliest thing Humphrey had ever seen and he couldn't get the image out of his mind.

"Hey! You all right?"

Deputy Humphrey was brought back to reality by the sound of Ben Something-or-other's voice. He had drifted off again, besieged by the morbid mental sight of Wendy Pullman's body.

"Yeah, I'm fine," Humphrey said. He checked his watch and shook his head. "To hell with it. Bring it in. We've been looking for two hours already."

Ben nodded, and the officer out with him seemed just as relieved as Ben. A chubby fellow named Swanson, he mopped his forehead with a handkerchief he pulled from his back pocket like the world's slowest magic trick.

Humphrey honestly hadn't expected to find another body here. Even if there *was* another one, he figured it would be somewhere else. The two bodies had been found in different parts of the woods, in different swamps. But they *had* both appeared to be gator attacks.

Appeared to be.

Ben brought the boat to the edge of the swamp, where the water and the land merged to create a sludge. Swanson got out with a grunt, and Ben followed.

"Thanks, Ben," Humphrey said.

"Sure thing. You look disappointed."

"I got two dead bodies on my hands. Of course I'm disappointed."

"Hey man, it's gators, right? Not much the po-po can do about that."

Humphrey sighed and shook his head. "You need help loading the boat back up?"

"Nah. I'm good. My truck's back over that-a-way," he said, hitching his thumb over his shoulder. "Figure I might fish for some crawdads before I take it out, anyway."

"Have fun."

Humphrey started walking back through the woods, a stretch that would lead him and Swanson back to the little dirt cutover they'd parked the car on.

"You know," Swanson said, "Ben said you look disappointed. But that ain't quite right. It's something else."

"Perplexed might be a better word."

"Why's that?"

"Two bodies. Two different spots in the woods. Chalking it up to gators seems too convenient. Especially when gators aren't spotted in this area very often."

"But they *are* spotted on occasion, right?"

"Yeah, they are."

"So what are you thinking?" Swanson asked in an accent that was somehow both very southern and very Creole.

"I'm thinking they may have been killed somewhere else and disposed of in the places they were found."

"Killed by gators?"

"I don't know. The Forestry Service says they've been especially ornery this season. But what I do know is that two dead bodies in four days, found in very isolated places...I'm going to follow protocol on this. Get the regional FBI on it, just in case."

They came out of the woods, the gnats having died off a bit. As they got back into the patrol car, Humphrey looked back out to the forest. He'd been on the force for eleven years now and so far had only heard of three people being attacked by gators, and only one of those people had died.

So, two in two days seemed like a bit much.

He let Swanson drive, opting to sit in the passenger seat and think it all through. What made more sense? The crazy odds of finding two bodies mauled by gators in two days, or someone killing the victims and dumping them elsewhere?

But how would a killer make it *look like* the victims had been gnawed on by gators?

Hell, he didn't know. He guessed it was a good idea the bureau would soon be involved.

CHAPTER THREE

Camille sat in a lounge-style chair in the waiting area, going through her approach in her head. She was about to pitch a tricky bit of business to a new director and it had the potential to go rather badly. She'd either come off as self-important and egotistical or eager and caring. Quite frankly, she wasn't sure if she wanted McCutcheon viewing her as any of these.

The visit to her father had been depressing, but surprisingly insightful. More than that, Camille had left his house with a feeling of confirmation. For years, she'd always wondered what it might be like to re-open her sister's case. She had no delusions about finding pleasing answers at the end of it, but that wasn't the reasoning behind it anyway. No, she simply wanted to provide Nanette with a sense of justice and closure, even if she *was* dead.

Of course, she'd never been confirmed dead. For nearly thirteen years now, she'd only been *missing*. With almost a decade of FBI work under her belt, Camille knew that this was an equation with a rather obvious answer. Someone that was missing for that long was either dead and undiscovered somewhere, or it was evidence of someone that had run away and *really* didn't want to be found.

All of this is what led her to the small waiting space outside of Assistant Director Marie McCutcheon's office the morning after visiting her father. Camille knew she couldn't just start looking into a case. She *might* have tried something so bold back in Alabama under her old director, but she didn't want to start this new chapter of her career on a bad foot.

McCutcheon finally entered the waiting area, walking quickly to her office. The woman was dressed in a dark pantsuit, but the sort of that looked tailored for power rather than appeasement. McCutcheon carried herself with more confidence than Camille had seen in any woman she'd ever met in the bureau. It was a feature that both impressed and terrified Camille.

Still, Assistant Director McCutcheon smiled at Camille as she reached her office door. She carried a cup of coffee in one hand and a thin stack of binders in the other.

"Good morning, Agent Grace," she said. "Would you mind grabbing the door for me?"

"Of course."

She opened the door and stepped to the side as McCutcheon entered. She then simply hovered there for a moment until AD McCutcheon waved her in. "Come on in. I assume you were here because you wanted to talk to me?"

"Thank you. And yes, I had something I wanted to ask you about if you have the time."

"I'm free for another fifteen minutes. That long enough?"

"Yes, I think it should be."

"Then have a seat," McCutcheon said as she took her own seat in a minimal-looking office chair, behind a neat yet somehow busy desk. Papers were scattered everywhere, but in an orderly way. She opened up her laptop, typed in a password, and then gave Camille her undivided attention while sipping on her coffee.

"Assistant Director, I wonder if you know everything about my history," Camille said as she sat down. "I know there are some details of it from my case files, but the entire story isn't there. I wonder if Director Milton out of Birmingham may have told you about my sister."

"Just the basics," McCutcheon said. "Milton was very protective of your privacy and told me only what I needed to know. I know your sister went missing when she was nineteen or so, correct? And she was never found."

"That's right. And while I've seen the reports and case files on her investigation, there were lots of areas for things to be improved upon. Lots of lazy work, if I'm being blunt." She paused here, giving McCutcheon an opportunity to respond, but she stayed quiet. Camille went on, speaking slowly and doing her best not to seem as if she was pleading. "I was curious if, while I'm getting my feet under me here, if you might allow to me re-open her case. It wouldn't be my main focus, but something I can work on discreetly when time allows. I have, of course, attempted to look into it on my own over the years, but never in an official capacity. Never with the use of FBI records and resources."

McCutcheon remained quiet for several seconds. Camille watched as she thought it over. She was relieved that she hadn't received an immediate *no* which, she knew, would have been fair. She knew it was a big request to make, especially because she hadn't even officially been on the job here in New Orleans for two weeks yet.

Finally, McCutcheon leaned forward bit and gave Camille a saddened look. "For now, it's going to be a no. And it has nothing to do with you or the case itself. I'm sure you understand that I can't have a new agent come in here and start requesting the cases they want to work on, even if it *is* in an almost unofficial capacity. And the fact that it concerns a family member of yours makes it even more controversial. However, I *will* say this: settle in here, put in the work, and show me and the other agents what a crucial cog you can be to the system. Get to that point and then we can discuss this again. Does that seem fair to you?"

"Of course," Camille said, trying to hide her disappointment. "I'm sorry I wasted your time with this."

"This isn't a waste of time, Camille. I'd like you to make yourself comfortable here."

"Well, thank you for hearing me out. I can only hope that you consider my request when the time is right."

"I'll do that."

Camille rose from her seat and made her way to the exit of McCutcheon's office. She had to force herself to not turn around and ask her to reconsider. She knew this had been a long shot, but a deep part of her still wanted to feel like she was doing something to find her sister. Though she knew in her heart that Nanette was most likely dead, she'd been unable to shake the thought that she was still out there somewhere.

At that same time, McCutcheon's desk phone rang. Not wanting to be any more of a bother, Camille gave a little wave of thanks and made her way out of the door. She made her way back through the waiting area as she heard McCutcheon on the phone. She did her best not to feel slighted over the decision that had been made. It did make sense, and she knew this, but it did not lessen the sting at all.

Camille had barely stepped out into the hallway when she heard McCutcheon calling her name from behind her. It was hardly audible from her office, through the waiting area, and out into the hall. Still, Camille doubled back quickly and, just twenty seconds after having exited, she stepped back into McCutcheon's office.

McCutcheon waved her in and pointed to the seat she'd just been occupying. Still speaking on the phone, the assistant director pressed a button on the phone's cradle, setting it to speaker mode. She then said: "Captain Beecher, I have Agent Camille Grace here, also on the call. Could you please repeat what you just told me?"

"Sure. Agent Grace, good to meet you. We've got two bodies out here in the town of Hen Creek, about fifteen miles south of Houma. Everything points to these deaths being gator attacks, but the locations being so spread apart and where the bodies were found doesn't really jive."

"Why's that?" Camille asked.

"Well, for example, with the most recent victim, the area where it was found doesn't get much gator activity. Hardly any, actually. If a gator *did* attack her, it would have dragged her body a ways...up to two miles or so. And that isn't very likely."

"I see," she said. And while she *did* see, she could also see where this conversation was headed. She glanced at McCutcheon, trying to get a read on her.

"Anyway," Captain Beecher said, "with two bodies that we can't *officially* say are gator attacks yet, we'd really like to get the feds down just to run a preliminary search. Shouldn't take too long. We just want to make sure we're doing it all by the book, you understand."

Before Camille could say anything else, McCutcheon took over. "Captain, if you'll email your reports and findings to this point, we'll get Agent Grace out that way by the end of the day."

Camille did her best to keep her face calm as McCutcheon gave her email address. She knew it was a bullshit assignment, the sort of thing that felt almost like a hazing. It made her wonder if McCutcheon's jovial mood and attitude with her so far had all been squashed when she'd asked about re-opening Nanette's case.

McCutcheon ended the call and gave Camille a stayed glance that was impossible to read. *Maybe I'm reading too much into it,* Camille thought. *Maybe it's a softball of an assignment that she just wants to give to the new agent that doesn't have a workload yet.*

"Hen Creek is only about an hour and fifteen minutes away. You think you can be there by eleven?"

"That shouldn't be a problem. You'll forward me whatever Captain Beecher sends you?"

"You'll have it immediately after it hits my inbox."

"Sounds good."

Without being formally dismissed, Camille stood up from the seat again and made her exit from AD McCutcheon's office for the second time within five minutes.

Somehow, she'd gone from asking to look into her sister's disappearance to going to take a look at possible alligator attacks. The speed in which it had all changed was dizzying but she supposed that was okay for now. After all, one of the reasons she'd moved out here, aside from feeling a long-buried connection to the place where she'd grown up, was to shake things up.

And if looking into what was very likely going to turn out to be nothing more than gator attacks wasn't considered *shaking things up*, then maybe she was simply never going to be happy.

CHAPTER FOUR

Special Agent Scott Palmer hurried into the FBI's New Orleans field office, arriving to work nearly ten minutes before he normally did. He was currently between cases, more or less seen as an errand boy until something big landed in his lap. So far, he had nothing on his agenda aside from assisting with wiretaps for a surveillance team trying to bust a coke dealer, and any research tasks sent his way. He didn't mind these kinds of lazy days, but it certainly wasn't why he'd been dreaming of being an agent since the age of eleven, when he'd watched his first episode of *The X-Files.*

He'd come in early because he was hoping to make it down to Camille Grace's office before he was due at a morning meeting. Four days had passed since he'd first heard that Camille had been transferred to the New Orleans field office. And by the time he'd caught wind of that news, she'd been on-site for at least two or three days.

He wasn't sure how to feel about her not reaching out to him. They'd closed a particularly grisly case concerning voodoo murders a little less than a month ago, when she had come down to assist out of Birmingham, Alabama. And when she'd left, they'd made the usual passing comments about how whenever one of them was in the other's neighborhood, they should reconnect. While Palmer knew this was always a formality, just something you said to an agent you respected, he felt that they'd both actually meant it.

And here she was, having been relocated to New Orleans, back to her old stomping grounds. She'd been here for at least a week and hadn't reached out. He supposed that could be because of several factors. First, maybe she wasn't quite moved in yet and wanted to make sure she had her feet firmly planted before dabbling in a social life. And the second option was that she simply didn't want to reach out. Palmer supposed he could have misread the situation when she'd left. Maybe the respect between them wasn't as mutual as he'd been thinking. Maybe she was purposefully avoiding him.

He planned to figure it out this morning. Even if it was a quick conversation to establish that she wasn't interested in venturing into a friendship, he needed to know. He'd be fine, really. He wasn't romantically interested in her. He'd simply enjoyed working with her and appreciated her approach to working a case.

So with that intention in mind, he waited for the elevators in the main lobby. He knew her office was downstairs, just from watercooler conversations he'd heard around the office. The building was mostly quiet, as the main surge of agents coming in for their morning shifts was still ten minutes away.

The elevator doors dinged as the car came to a stop. The door slid open and as he stepped inside, his leg stopped for just a moment, and a smile came to his face.

Camille Grace was in the elevator, stepping out. She looked surprised to see him and, he was delighted to see, smiled right back at him.

"Agent Grace," he said.

"Agent Palmer," she responded. "How have you been?"

"Can't complain. But I have to admit...I was on my way down to see you."

"Oh yeah?"

"Yeah. I heard you'd been relocated here—that you've been here for a few days."

Her cringe told him that she knew where he was taking this. She nodded and offered him a shrug. "It's been a very weird week. I knew you worked out of this office, of course. I thought about hunting you down, but trust me...I would have been awful company to have this past week or so."

"I get it. Working out of a new place can be the pits, right?"

"That, and then some family stuff."

Palmer nodded, recalling how sensitive she was over her tumultuous family history. It seemed odd to him that her family might have been one of the reasons she had decided to come back out to New Orleans if she was so touchy about that subject. All of that, though, was not his business so he decided to leave it untouched.

"Have you settled in yet?" he asked.

"I have. The downstairs office is pretty nice. I do feel like the dirty secret McCutcheon is trying to hide, but it's nice all the same."

"Are you headed out for the day?" he asked.

"I am. I was just handed a...well, I guess you could call it a case." She shrugged, an annoyed look clouding her face. "I'm being sent out to Hen Creek to verify that two dead bodies were indeed killed by gators and not by a murderer."

"Sounds better than what I've got going on. I'm between cases, helping with wiretapping. So I get to listen to three or four guys talk about their exaggerated sexual exploits, and why they're thinking the Saints are going to tank this season."

"Ouch. Well, hey, they can't all be gator cases," she said with a smile. "You know, Palmer...give me another couple of days. Let's plan to hang out sometime. Maybe grab a drink or something."

"Yeah," he said, though his mind was already elsewhere. Gators...the little shit-splat town of Hen Creek. That could make for a nice little field trip. If he could get AD McCutcheon to sign off on it. "I wonder, though...what about today?"

"What about it?"

"Would you like some company?"

"Please don't take offense to this, but my task is to literally see if these people were killed by gators or not. I think I can handle it alone."

"Yes, but I'm being selfish. Let me rephrase it. If I can get out of my crap duty and McCutcheon will let me, would you mind if I tagged along?"

"You think she'll let you?"

"Yes. Out there in Hen Creek, it can get pretty medieval. Racist, sexist, all of that. The PD, even if it's the state, isn't going to bend all that much for a female agent. I also have a working relationship with the sheriff out there."

"Then why didn't she just send you?"

"She may be testing you. Maybe to see if you sort of stiffen up at a case that seems beneath you. All the better for me to come, if you ask me. I'll have to paint it in a way that I'm volunteering to assist you. Maybe even mention how well you and I worked together on that voodoo case. And if she says no, then no harm, no foul. We'll meet up for that drink in a few days."

He watched as Camille considered it for a moment, ending her contemplation with a shrug. "If you can make it happen, sure. I'd love to have you. You don't have much time, though. I'm due to show up on-site by eleven."

Palmer checked his watch, though he already knew the time. It was 8:27; he'd come in early, hoping to catch Camille, after all.

"Grab a coffee at the shop on the corner," he said. "I'll either see you in about fifteen minutes, or text you to let you know you'll be touring gator country on your own."

"Okay," she said. Palmer wasn't totally sure, but he thought she looked pleased with the idea of having his company.

He watched Camille start across the lobby, to the front doors. Not wanting to seem too interested and needy, he then finally stepped on the elevator and rode it up, hoping his arguments for accompanying Camille would come across as strongly as they'd sounded downstairs.

CHAPTER FIVE

Camille was trying to figure out if Palmer was just a really good bullshitter or if McCutcheon respected him enough to give in to his wishes. Whatever the case, he met her at the coffee shop exactly fourteen minutes after they parted ways at the elevator.

Palmer elected to drive the sixty-eight miles between the field office and Hen Creek, which was fine with Camille. It gave her an opportunity to look over the case files Captain Beecher had sent over. It honestly wasn't much to see. There were a few photos that backed up the gator theory quite easily. To an untrained eye, the photos and the depictions of the scenes where the bodies were found did indeed seem like unfortunate cases of alligators attacking humans.

There were two peculiar items that nagged at Camille, though. First of all, the victims were quite varied. A young woman and a middle-aged man, meaning there was no obvious preference for the type of victim. She supposed this actually supported the gator-attack theory. Gators, after all, likely didn't discriminate.

Still, with both victims, why they would have been out in the forest, deep in the thickets and swamps, made no immediate sense. Secondly, from what she could see in the photos (which weren't professionally captured by any means), she could see no signs of a struggle. And she imagined getting ensnared by a gator would cause someone to struggle like hell up to the point of their death.

When she was done with the notes, discussing them sporadically with Palmer, she took a moment to look out of the window. As they drew closer to Hen Creek, more of the rural area started to present itself. While it was in the opposite direction of her hometown of Upping, it looked very much the same. Dark green stretches of forest, invasive kudzu everywhere, little mom-and-pop shops and diners here and there. It was a far cry from Bourbon Street and the French Quarter, that was for sure.

It was like a different world out here, a world she'd once known but now felt alien to her. Every house tuckering back off of the road in overgrown grass, every truck up on blocks, was like a ghost from her past, welcoming her back.

Not wanting to get bogged down in her emotions, she looked away from the poor, rural surroundings. She pulled down her visor, flipped up the little flap inside, and looked herself over in the mirror.

She had not once caught Palmer checking her out and she honestly wasn't usually the sort to fret over her looks. All the same, it was her first case out of the New Orleans office and she wanted to make a good impression. And if these men out in Hen Creek were the way Palmer had suggested, she figured she'd try to kick their asses every way she knew how.

Her standard black slacks were somewhat form fitting and the jacket covering her blouse wasn't exactly flattering. Not that it mattered; it was going to be humid out today and they'd likely spend most of it out in the woods. She figured she'd probably leave the stupid jacket in the car. Her long, straight dark hair was in a ponytail, and a few wisps of it had snuck out and framed her face. She looked good today, even she had to admit it—which was hard for her to do.

A small sign for Hen Creek appeared on the right side of the road. Almost immediately behind it was a tacky-looking road sign advertising airboat tours and fishing guides.

"I guess gator attacks aren't a good thing for the air boating industry, huh?" Palmer joked.

Using GPS, they navigated to the address Captain Beecher had sent over. It was a sketchy-looking dirt road that led through an overground field. In the back of the field, almost as if plopped there as an afterthought, was a rugged cabin. Two vehicles were parked there: a battered old pickup truck and a police car.

As they drew closer to the cabin down a dirt road that had the merest bit of gravel in it, Camille saw a small sign over the door. HEN CREEK AIRBOATS.

"Christ Almighty," she said. "Are we going out on airboats?"

"I sort of hope so," Palmer said. "This is *so* much better than the day I originally had lined up."

He parked behind the police car. When they stepped out into the growing Louisiana heat, Camille heard two voices and a bit of banging around coming from behind the little cabin. They made their way around the back and found two men standing around an old airboat. One of the men was dressed in a dingy navy t-shirt and a pair of camouflage shorts. The other was dressed in a standard police uniform. He was an older man, maybe a bit north of fifty, with a mostly-gray five o' clock shadow on his plump cheeks.

"Captain Beecher?" Camille asked as she and Palmer stepped into view.

The cop turned away from the airboat and Camille saw by the nameplate over his left breast pocket that this was not Beecher. The plate read HUMPHREY, and the badge he wore on his uniform indicated that he was not a captain, but a deputy.

"Nope, sorry," Humphrey said. He walked over to greet them, extending his hand right. "Deputy Rick Humphrey. And damn, I gotta say that you folks got here quick."

Camille shook his hand first. "Agent Camille Grace. And yes, I figured we may as well knock this out as quickly as we can."

Palmer stepped forward and introduced himself as well, shaking Humphrey's hand.

Palmer nodded to the beat-up airboat. The cage that housed the propeller on the back was dented and busted open in two spots. The fiberglass body looked as if it were about a century old, the colors long ago faded.

"I hope we're not taking this," Palmer said.

"No, not at all," Humphrey said. He then gestured to the man in the t-shirt and shorts—a muscular, shaggy-looking man of about thirty or so. "This is Ben. he helps run this little airboat company. I believe I've caught him trying to take the engine out to use in another boat."

"That about sums it up," Ben said, stepping away from the boat with a look of frustration. He wore an old, tattered baseball cap, which he removed long enough to wipe sweat from his brow. When he turned his attention to the agents, his eyes lingered a bit too long on Camille. "Ben Givens," he said. "Good to meet you both."

"Ben is going to take us to the site where the most recent body was found. I had you meet me here because the only other way to the scene involves a mile-long walk through the woods. Also, if a gator *did* get these folks, I figure it might help to see the water route it likely took in order to get to them."

"Do you think it was gators, Deputy?" Camille said.

"I almost *hope* it was. Because the alternative isn't much better. But that's why you're here, right?"

"Right. But still...what's your gut telling you?"

Humphrey shrugged and looked to the ground. "I think it looks like a gator attack right down to the last detail. But the locations don't make sense, which makes me think someone *really* wanted it to look like a gator did it. But I hate to make that assumption, you know?"

Camille nodded and then looked to the rear of the field. She saw a small trail back there, coming back around to the far left side of the cabin. She assumed it led to a creek or a river—the avenue they'd be taking to the site.

"Well, then," she said, "let's go have a look."

***

Camille had ridden on an airboat just twice in her life, both times during her childhood in Upping. Both instances had been while she'd been spending weekends with Deanna. A friend of hers had owned two of them, one for casual rides around the bayous and swamps, the other purely for fishing purposes.

The one Ben Givens had selected for their trip down the river was rather nice. He didn't have the engine opened up nearly all the way, but even the slight speed he was pushing was a sign to Camille that this craft was capable of some serious speed.

She tried to keep track of where they were, watching the bayou landscape speed by. It was both stagnant and beautiful all at the same time, the dark trees casting shadows in a dizzying display.

She took it all on, enjoying the feel of the wind against her and scenery that surprisingly calmed her. If this *was* indeed meant to be sort of a hazing case, it had backfired. She was remarkably at peace for a moment.

That was, until Ben pointed ahead, yelling a warning back to her, Palmer, and Deputy Humphrey.

"Gators."

He said it as if it had simply started misting rain, like it was really no big deal. Her eyes followed the direction he was pointing and she watched as a gator made its way up a muddy bank and into the thick, green brush to their left. In the water just below, another one remained in the water. The top of its head broke the surface, and a small fraction of its tail was curled up on the bank.

"Those aren't considered big ones, are they?" Palmer asked.

"Nah, not too bad," Humphrey said. "But really, they bigger ones aren't typically found in this part of the state."

Camille, having grown up in an area where alligators weren't the norm but were spotted from time to time knew a decent amount about them. She knew enough to understand that they didn't tend to attack or charge unless you were right up on them and even then, they had to be having a bad, irritable day.

Still, seeing them so close while on a case that may or may not involve them was a bit eerie.

They continued on, Ben navigating the airboat expertly down the river even as it grew slightly thinner and shallower. After ten minutes or so of driving down the river, Ben slowed the craft and pulled it into a nook about fifty feet from the water. The copse of trees there was so thick that Camille assumed that Ben had to know where exactly to turn in order to open up enough room to pull the craft in. It bobbed slightly as the front end touched the bank.

Deputy Humphrey stepped down first, reaching up like a gentleman to help Camille down. Though she did not need the assistance, she took his hand and let him help her down to the ground. Camille stepped down from the airboat onto the muddy earth that was devoid of any weeds. She was glad to see no gators.

Palmer and Ben came down next. Ben anchored the airboat by trying a rope to a post along the front of the boat and then to a nearby bald cypress.

They walked through the tree line, approximately thirty feet wide but extending for miles on either side of the boat. The ground was soft, the sort of soil that nearly swallowed her shoe with each step.

The four of them made their way through the dense forest with Humphrey leading the way. A cloud of gnats started to hover around their heads and Camille started to smell the overly-earthy scents of swampier land ahead. The walk didn't take long; coming in on the airboat had apparently helped much more than Humphrey had let on. After walking just three minutes, he brought the small group to a stop at the treacherous banks of what looked like nothing more than an enormous mud hole. The water ventured back further into the forest for an unseen distance, covered in a canopy of trees so thick that the sun barely touched them or the water at all.

There were small movements in the water as all manner of insects and rugged aquatic life darted back and forth. A large bullfrog croaked nearby and even as they stood there, Camille watched a small, black snake slither underneath a log no more than a dozen or so feet from where Ben Givens stood.

"The body of the second victim, thirty-six-year-old Wendy Pullman, was found here," Humphrey said. "Two boys were out just messing around in the woods and saw the body. She was no more than three feet out."

Camille took another step towards the black water and squatted down to get a better look at the ground. She saw a few prints along the rim of the water: a few that looked like deer, another that might have been a fox. What she absolutely did not see was any indication that a gator had been here anytime recently.

"Anyone know about how heavy an average gator is?" she asked without looking away from the ground.

Ben answered, his voice quiet and reserved. It was almost as if he was showing respect to the area because a dead body had been found there.

"An average male, full grown, is going to weight anywhere between five hundred and seven hundred pounds. But even smaller ones—smaller ones capable of dragging a body around, mind you—are still going to register around two or three hundred."

"I know what you're thinking," Humphrey said. "Not a single track. Those fox tracks you see right there...those were here when I was here yesterday. And a fox doesn't weigh much at all. Maybe fifty or sixty pounds if it's full grown. Now, there's always the chance that the gator could have come in through the backside of this mess but we've checked over there, too. There's no indication that a gator has been in this area at all anytime in the recent past."

"I can take y'all over there if you want," Ben said.

Camille thought it might be a good idea for the sake of thoroughness, but she could tell from Humphrey's tone and expression that he knew it would be a waste of time. She looked to Palmer, who also had eyes down on those tracks in the soft mud.

"What do you think?" she asked.

"I don't think we need to see it. What I do think is that we need to find out more about the victims. We need to find out if there was *any* reason at all Ms. Pullman might have been out here or anywhere else gators might be."

"I've been working on contacting the families, letting them know the FBI might be coming by," he said. "They all think it's stupid because as far as they can see, their loved ones were attacked by alligators. And hell, for all we know, that might very well be the case."

"What about the boys?" Camille asked.

"Nah, I have no suspicion at all that they're involved."

"I mean what about questioning them?" Camille said. "I'd like to know everything they saw that day, from the moment they came into the woods until the police arrived."

"I can arrange that pretty quickly," Humphrey said. "As a matter of fact, one of them lives no more than two miles away from here."

"I say we start there," Camille said.

"Same," Palmer agreed.

Humphrey nodded and led them back out away from the swamp. But before Camille turned away, she stared back out to it. The water, so black and dirty, was almost like an oil spill. It looked almost evil, like the perfect place to hide a secret.

CHAPTER SIX

Camille was slightly unnerved by just how easy it was for her to find a sense of familiarity and peace to the unmarked back roads that wound through the rural and swamp-riddled areas of Louisiana. Dark stretches of pavement, some even without the white and yellow lines along the sides and center, leading deeper into forests so dense and dark green that it was almost like another world.

She and Palmer followed behind Humphrey, a black sedan tailing a Hen Creek patrol car. They'd been quiet for most of the ride, but the silence was broken when Palmer let out a deep sigh from behind the steering wheel.

"Something bothering you?" she asked, rolling her eyes at the dramatic nature of the sigh.

"I'm just wondering how pissed McCutcheon is going to be if this thing takes more than a day."

"Are you also thinking it's doubtful that it was gators?"

"Actually, I'm pretty sure it *was* gators. But I get the sense that you don't."

"I think stating it's gators and then leaving town would be a little lazy. Right now, I'd say the scenes themselves don't hint at gators."

"I don't think the scenes themselves matter," Palmer argued. Ahead of them, Humphrey put on his left blinker and turned down a small, dirt driveway. "I mean, there's a decent amount of swamp around here. Who's to say the bodies weren't killed by gators elsewhere and just floated to the locations where they were found?"

The thought had also crossed Camille's mind, but the absence of tracks and any sign of struggle was still tickling at her suspicions.

They came to the end of the dirt driveway, parking beside Deputy Humphrey's car. The house ahead of them was a simple one-story home, the sort with a raised concrete slab for a porch and white siding that looked nearly beige from dust and grime having collected over the years.

They got out of the car and Camille took a deeper look around as they approached the front porch. The yard was little more than patches of dirt and dead grass, adorned with the occasional flowering weed.

Humphrey knocked and almost right away, they could hear the sound of footsteps from inside. They were hurrying to the door and Camille could feel the vibrations on the porch. She didn't think it had anything to do with the size of the person that was approaching the door, but more with the age and construction of the house.

When the door was opened, a thin, pretty woman of about forty or so greeted them. She eyed the trio with a bit of suspicion but her eyes eased when they found Humphrey.

"Deputy, how are you?" she asked.

"Just fine, thanks," Humphrey said. "Tammy, I want to introduce you to Agents Palmer and Grace, out of New Orleans. They're here just to sort of dot the i's and cross the t's on this gator case. I was hoping you'd allow them to talk to Donald about what he saw."

"I guess that would be fine, but he already told two different cops about it—even one from the State."

Camille stepped forward and offered a smile. "It's really just a formality, ma'am. We'd like to get a better understanding of the scene as the boys came upon it."

It was clear that Tammy didn't like the idea of FBI agents rolling up in her house, but she stepped aside. "Yeah, I reckon that's fine. Just don't push him too hard. He's having a hard time with it. Nightmares and all."

"Of course not," Camille said. "Thank you."

Tammy led them into her home, a modest little place that showed the signs of meticulous cleaning and care.

"Donnie!" Tammy called out into the house, looking down the short hall to their right. "Come on out here! There are some folks that need to talk to you."

Tammy never offered for them to sit down, so Camille remained on her feet. She supposed Humphrey had already been here, as he wasted no time taking seat on the couch as they waited.

Just a few seconds later, a boy of about eleven or twelve stepped out into the hallway and entered the room. He saw Camille and Palmer and looked confused.

Palmer nodded to Donnie and said, "Hey there, Donald. I'm Agent Palmer, with the FBI. And this is my partner, Agent Grace. We just need a few minutes of your time to ask you about the afternoon you found the body out in the swamp."

"We know you've already been over it a few times," Camille said almost apologetically. "But if you could just run us through it one more time, we'd appreciate it."

Donnie seemed to relax a bit over this. Camille wondered if the boy liked being the center of attention—feeling the cops and now even the FBI were interested in what he had to say.

"Sure," he said, glancing over to his mother. She stood at the area where the living room connected with a small dining room, watching the scene unfold as if she didn't quite trust them.

"Honestly," Palmer said, "all we need to know is what you saw in the moments leading up to when you got to the swamp. Just before you saw the body. Did you happen to see anything weird or maybe out of place? Any movement in the woods?"

"No, sir," Donnie said. "It was just a normal day, you know? The same old bugs and stuff, but that was about it."

"Do you think you can describe the minute or two that passed before you found the body?" Camille asked.

"Sure. There's not much to tell, though. We were just walking along, me and PJ. We were going to just dip our toes in the water. I know it's stupid, but we thought it would make a cool story for when we went back to school. The swamp out there, it sort of comes out of nowhere, you know? Even for us, we knew it was going to start any minute, you know? And we still almost fell in. Anyway, I put my foot in and we were joking that it wasn't too bad, that we should even go out to our knees. And I was about to do that when I saw the dead woman. Well, I sort of felt her first…with my leg when I was in the water."

Camille was impressed with the level of detail, but it wasn't what she was looking for.

"Do you remember if there were any weird tracks out there? Anything at all? Maybe shoe prints, or animal tracks?"

"No ma'am. Nothing like that. But we weren't...I mean we weren't really looking out for anything like that."

Camille nodded, also recalling that the initial police reports had specifically stated there had been no prints at the scene despite the ground being muddy. The only prints at all had been the shallow ones the boys had left behind.

"And when you boys came rushing back home, you didn't see anyone sort of lurking around out by the swamp, either?"

"No ma'am. Nothing like that."

Camille had spoken to enough kids and teens during cases to know when there wasn't going to be any sort of pay off. There was nothing here for them, no matter how precise and detailed Donnie got.

She allowed Palmer to ask a few follow-up questions, but she knew they were done here. She did see the signs of trauma in Donnie's eyes as he recalled the evening that he and his friend had stumbled across the body. Camille had seen the pictures in the files and even through her phone screen, she could tell the body had been in rough shape, not just because of the gator attack, but the exposure to the swamp, the heat, and countless bugs. She felt bad for the kids and almost wished they'd never even come by here to question him.

Palmer wrapped up and they left the house less than ten minutes after arriving. Camille, Palmer, and Humphrey huddled at their cars and she could sense the listless sort of acceptance coming from the men. She knew that if they didn't find some sort of evidence of foul play soon, the case would end up being listed as an alligator attack. So she was going to have to choose her next steps wisely.

"Deputy, the police report said the next of kin that was immediately contacted after the second body was discovered was the mother. How close is she to here?"

"Close. Everyone that lives in Hen Creek is pretty much on top of one another."

"You think she'd be up to talking?"

"Possibly. Wendy Pullman had her mother living with her. A seventy-one-year-old woman with a long list of medical problems. I think she was fine in accepting that her daughter had been killed by a gator, so I don't know how she'd handle the FBI asking questions and shaking things up. But she seems like the helpful type. Might be worth a visit."

"I think I'd like to go by there."

"Well then, I can give you the address. I need to get back to the station for a bit. But you're welcome to call me with any questions."

"Actually, I was wondering if you could call the coroner for us," Camille said. She noticed Palmer bristling beside her, clearly not expecting such a request. "Let them know we'll be by in a bit so they can have the paperwork ready for us to look over."

Humphrey seemed surprised at this, too, but in an almost impressed sort of way. "Yeah, I can do that."

With that, Humphrey gave them Wendy Pullman's address, an address that was now solely her mother's. He then bid them farewell and pulled away in his cruiser.

"Okay," Palmer said as they got back into their car. "I'm very glad to be out of the office and wire-tapping but I do need to say that I think maybe you're trying too hard on this one. If it looks like a gator and smells like a gator, it's likely a gator."

"Give me the mom and the coroner's visit," Camille said. "If nothing out of either of those visits changes your mind, I'll concede to that. Let's not forget," she said with a grin, "that you're really just a tag-along on this one.

"That's a fair deal," he said, starting the engine and backing out of the driveway. "And also…ouch."

Once again, they headed down back roads that felt like home to her. As Palmer drove, she looked out at the forest and realized that while it clearly wasn't as thick and as dangerous as say, the Amazon, it still held its own particular sets of dangers. And considering that, she couldn't help but wonder if maybe Palmer was right. Maybe she was trying too hard. Maybe she was wanting to make this case more than it actually was so she could prove herself to McCutcheon.

Only time would tell, she supposed. And with only two more stops to make before she and Palmer seriously discussed closing the case and heading home, the whole case started to feel so much more important.

CHAPTER SEVEN

Camille pulled the car along the curb of the Pullman residence, feeling that this particular moment was the official start to the case. Wendy Pullman had lived in a cute brick house that sat on a hill just off the road. The lawn was green, the driveway was lined with gravel, and the flowerbeds looked to have been greatly cared for. The backdrop of the forest and the swamps remained, though, bordering the yard almost like a reminder of where they were living.

Given that they were dealing with not only a woman that had just lost a daughter, but an older lady with several medical issues according to Humphrey, Camille took the lead. She knocked on the front door as bees buzzed in the flowerbeds behind them. It took about thirty seconds for Mrs. Pullman to come to the door. It opened slowly and the face that greeted them looked puffy, tired, and sad.

"Mrs. Pullman?" Camille asked.

"Yes, I'm Sue Pullman. Who are you?"

"I'm Agent Grace and this is my partner, Agent Palmer. We're in town to assist the local police with matters concerning your daughter and another potentially related case."

"The FBI is looking into gator attacks?" she asked doubtfully. "Isn't that more of a thing for the game warden?"

"Typically, yes. But as I said, there have been two victims in less than a week and we want to make sure the deaths can be safely attributed to gators."

"Just a formality," Palmer said from behind Camille. "Would you mind if we came inside and asked you a few questions?"

"Yes, I suppose so. The house is a mess, mind you."

Sue Pullman led them into a dimly lit hallway and then into the kitchen. Camille smelled baking bread and some sort of tomato-based sauce.

"Can I get you something to drink?" Sue asked. "I also have some fresh bread I just took out of the oven. I'm finding out that I like to cook and bake when grieving."

Palmer smiled warmly and said, "I'd love to try the bread."

Sue smiled and walked slowly to the kitchen counter which was littered with a variety of ingredients and measuring cups.

"Mrs. Pullman, I understand you're grieving," Camille said. "And I'm so very sorry for your loss. We'll make this a quick visit, I promise. We really just wanted to ask some questions about your daughter. We're trying to determine why she may have been out in those woods in the first place. In those woods, near the river, the swamps...anywhere out in the forests, really."

"Well," Sue said, slicing into a fresh loaf of bread. "It's a good question and one I can't figure out. I'd bet you anything that Wendy hadn't been out in the woods since she was a little girl chasing butterflies and moths."

"Can you maybe describe her to us?" Palmer asked as Sue brought his slice of bread over on a paper plate.

"She was a sweet girl. Very smart, but quiet. She always kept to herself. She went to college in New Orleans, got a degree in marine biology. She had some interviews lined up in Florida but then I got sick and she dropped it all to care for me."

"How long had you been living with her?"

"About four months now. One of the jobs down in Florida sort of panned out. She'd been able to do some stuff remotely. She...well I guess she won't get to do any of it anymore. The hope was that I'd turn around, you know? That I'd get healthy, and Wendy could resume her life."

"Do you mind me asking what you're sick with?" Camille asked.

"Cardiomyopathy. Tack that on top of my diabetes and it got sort of bad. Most days I feel really well, but when it's bad, it's *really* bad. I'd been in and out of the hospital two times in the last six weeks. And when the cops came and told me about what had happened..."

She trailed off, as if not wanting to risk having further complications by torturing herself over the sad facts concerning her daughter.

"You said she was quiet," Palmer said. "A bit of an introvert, but was there anyone she was close to? Any friends, anything like that?"

"She had a few friends, but she didn't really like to get involved with them. She was very much a homebody...which is why I think she was so open to having me move in with her. Even as a kid, she didn't seem to enjoy playdates. She was really into her books and her animals. She was always getting some new fish to put in her little aquarium and *boy* did she care for that thing."

"Was she ever married?" Camille asked.

"No. She was dating a boy in college and I was sure that's where it was leading, but it never happened."

"What about recently? No romantic interest?"

"No, she had a couple guys that she dated here and there but she never really got excited over anyone. I was sort of joking with her the other day...about a week or so ago, in fact. She'd started using one of those dating apps. That's where the few recent dates had come from."

Camille noted this and filed it away. A dating app was an open door to a variety of different options. Especially for a woman that was as introverted as Wendy Pullman seemed to have been.

"Can you think of anyone who'd want to hurt her?" Palmer asked. "Anyone that would have a grudge against her?"

"Oh no. I don't...wait. Wait. Why are you asking me these things? Are you thinking it *wasn't* an alligator?"

"We have no real reason to think it wasn't," Camille said. "But as I said, certain conditions over the past week here in Hen Creek have us out here to just make certain. It's really just protocol."

Sue nodded but seemed uncertain.

"She majored in marine biology," Palmer said. "So, you remember her ever saying anything about the swamps around here? Anything about the gators specifically?"

"No, I'm sorry. In fact, she hated the swamps. I believe her main interest in marine biology was coral reefs, habitats, things like that."

Camille continued to file these items away. And while they'd gotten a bit of information from Sue, Camille started to get that same inkling she'd felt with Donnie; they'd gotten all of the information they were going to get here.

She let Palmer wrap up again, noting that his charm and his compliments on the fresh baked bread were putting Sue at ease. It also helped her to see Palmer in a different light. From an outsider's perspective, his sarcasm and untouchable facade might suggest a man that was cold and distant. But she'd seen otherwise today.

Camille allowed him a few more moments before announcing that they needed to leave. And when she thought about venturing to the coroner's office next and the body that waited for them there, Camille was very glad she'd not asked for a piece of Sue Pullman's bread.

CHAPTER EIGHT

The coroner's office was located in Houma, a twenty minute drive away from the dense isolation of Hen Creek. As Camille and Palmer walked to the front doors, she could tell that Palmer was a little detached from the case. Based on his questions both before and during their visit with Sue Pullman, he'd given the impression that he believed the deaths to be the cause of alligators.

Camille, however, remained not so sure. It was more than her own leanings; she was also referring back to the doubt that Humphrey had shown. It was a doubt he'd never outright admitted to, but was evident in the way he approached their visit to the site.

After showing their badges at the front desk, they were escorted by a middle-aged man to the back of the building where the examination rooms were all lined up against a back wall. They were led into the one on the far right, where a woman wearing a protective dress apron stood at cleaned examination table. A gurney sat behind her, a sheet draped over a shape that was unmistakably a body.

"Agents Grace and Palmer, I assume?" she said. The woman shook their hands and made quick introductions. "I'm Stephanie Brooks, one of the primary county's coroners. Deputy Humphrey told me you'd be coming. You had questions about the recent gator attacks?"

"That's right," Camille said. "We're really just here to confirm they were indeed alligator attacks."

"Well, I've got all of the paperwork right here," Brooks said, turning and retrieving a thin stack of papers from the counter behind her. "If you don't mind my saying so, it seemed pretty cut and dry to me."

Camille took the papers and looked them over. The reports gave very minimal details on the deaths of Wendy Pullman as well as the first victim, a fifty-one-year-old man named Earl Stewart. All of the injuries to both victims had been easily evident. Wendy Pullman had been found with a good portion of her left leg stripped to the bone. She'd also been missing three fingers on her left hand and had a sizable chunk of meat taken from her right shoulder.

Even in the pictures, she could see where there were clear indications of what appeared to be bite marks, especially in the shoulder.

"This may sound like a dumb question," Camille said, "but what would you list as the cause of death, aside from something as basic as *gator attack*?"

"I imagine she bled out," Brooks said. "The damage her leg took on would have easily caused enough blood loss for her to bleed to death."

"Were there any signs of shock?"

"I'd imagine there were, but it looks like her body was out in the elements for at least two days. Any indicators of shock would now be worn down to the point of being hard to detect. As you can imagine, the heat did a number on her."

Camille nodded as she read over the rest of the reports. There was hardly anything there. Apparently, everyone involved with this case seemed perfectly fine closing the books on it and filing it away as a gator attack. The reports were lazy and substandard. There were no real details, just the most basic information filled in. It was as if someone had lazily written up the report while rushing through their lunchbreak. If she'd handed in something like this at the bureau, she'd have her ass handed to her.

"Is that Wendy Pullman?" Camille asked, nodding to the shape under the sheet behind Brooks.

"It is."

"What about Earl Stewart?"

"The funeral home has him. But I assure you, I did a thorough job. Mr. Stewart died because an alligator gnawed into his abdomen and took a bite out of his throat. The pictures are right there."

They were. And they were grisly. She was rather glad the body wasn't there.

"I'd like to see Ms. Pullman, please."

Next to her, she could hear Palmer grating under his breath: "Ah, Jesus, Grace. Really?"

Ignoring him, Camille walked to the smaller table behind Brooks as she removed the cloth. Wendy Pullman's body was revealed and it was rough to look at. Still, Camille did her best, trying to remain as professional as possible as she looked the body over. The wounds that had allegedly been made by an alligator had been closed up as neatly as they could, but the state of the rest of the body was still a challenge to take in.

Her skin had gone puffy and the exposure to the dank, muddy water of the swamp looked to have started eating away at her hands and feet. Brooks had done her best to tidy the areas up, but the damage was evident.

"What exactly are you looking for, Agent Grace?" Brooks asked.

"I'm just trying to gauge the evidence," Camille said. She moved around the table, taking in the entirety of it. Brooks had done a fine job of making the body a bit more presentable, but Camille doubted she'd been professional enough to notice anything out of the ordinary. She hated to assume something like that about a stranger, but she'd seen all she needed to see in the state of the lackluster reports.

"She's been autopsied, correct?" Camille asked.

"Of course."

"What did you find?"

"Nothing out of the ordinary," Brooks said. "She'd ingested some of the swamp water and there were insect larvae in her throat and stomach. But that was the only uncommon thing."

Camille noticed the slight edge of frustration in the coroner's voice at Camille's continued questions. Camille did her best to be patient.

"Okay so," Camille said, "if this was a gator attack and it ate her leg off then it would have been a big gator, right?"

"Most likely," Brooks said. "And there are some pretty big ones lurking around in this area." She studied Camille for a moment and let out a sigh. "Look, I don't really see you having any other option but to list it as an alligator attack. Certainly, there is nothing to indicate anything else."

"What about the other body?" Camille asked. "I've read the report. But when you examined the body, was there anything else you thought about?"

As Camille came to Wendy Pullman's right leg, she paused. Beside it, the bone of the left leg glistened white under the lights of the examination room. But Camille didn't notice. Instead, she focused on the right leg, just below the calf.

"Ms. Brooks, can I have a set of gloves?"

"What?"

"Gloves, please."

Brooks made no attempt to hide the fact that the request irritated her, but she retrieved a pair of latex gloves from a drawer along the bottom of the counter space. Camille slapped them on and gently lifted up the bottom portion of Wendy's leg. A bruise roughly the size of the grip-end of a baseball bat stood out, lighter now that she'd lost so much blood and had stopped breathing.

"I assume you saw this?" Camille said.

"I did."

"It wasn't listed in the paperwork."

"Because it's not relevant to the case. That bruise could have been picked up anywhere. It could have been one of the many smaller damages from the attack."

Yet, it's not in your report, Camille thought. But rather than argue further, she stepped away and allowed Brooks to cover the body back up again.

"I'd like to have the body moved to New Orleans and looked over by another coroner, if you don't mind."

"You...you what?" Brooks asked.

"We were sent to make sure these deaths were the result of alligator attacks. To make that call, I need detailed results. And right now, there aren't any to be had."

Brooks looked furious at first but then shrugged. "Whatever you want, agents."

"I'll make the call to get things initiated," Camille said. Then, speaking as warmly as she could, she added: "Thank you for your time, Ms. Brooks."

Brooks said nothing as Camille and Palmer left the examination room. Back out in the hallway and then passing the front desk again, Palmer chuckled.

"You don't care much about making friends, do you?" he asked.

"Not while on the job, no."

"You really think there's something else to these deaths, don't you?"

"My gut says yes. I think there's good chance they were killed and then dumped somewhere where alligators might have access to them."

"And then...what? The killer moved them again? If a killer was trying to dispose of bodies, wouldn't it just be easier to leave the bodies where the gators are? Seems like a pretty ideal way to get rid of a body if you ask me."

"I think you may be on to something there," she noted as they got into the car.

"Oh, and I noticed something else, too," Palmer said.

"Yeah?"

"You said you wanted to talk to Mrs. Pullman and then the coroner. And if there was nothing fishy, we'd head home. But you pissing off

Brooks and having the body moved...you sort of pulled the rug out from under me. You didn't go back on your word, but you manipulated the situation."

"Maybe," Camille said with a smile.

"I'm not mad about it, but...damn. You're good."

"I appreciate that. But let's save the flatter for when my gut turns out to be right."

Palmer pulled the car to the end of the parking lot and looked at the road. "Okay. Where to now?"

"The address for the first victim is in the case files. I think we should speak with his wife."

Palmer nodded in a defeated sort of way, still not entirely convinced. But as Camille started reciting directions to him from her GPS, he didn't complain. In fact, if Camille didn't know better, she thought he might be starting to feel a little stirring of suspicion in his guts, too.

CHAPTER NINE

Earl Stewart had lived just outside of Hen Creek, in an area that somehow appeared even more rural. His house was located on a lonely stretch of backroad that was heavily populated by thickets of trees, kudzu, and not much else. Oddly enough, though, the Stewart residence was quite beautiful. It had an older look to it and though Camille knew very little about architecture, she thought she could see some Colonial influence. It sat about fifty yards off the road. A lush, green yard was all that separated it from the road.

When Camille knocked on the door, they were greeted by a woman of about fifty-five. She looked haggard but also had the sort of face that Camille knew would be striking when a little makeup was applied.

"Yes?" she asked, eyeing Camille and Palmer with a tired sort of interest.

"Are you Nan Stewart?"

"I am."

"Ma'am, we're Agents Grace and Palmer with the FBI. We were hoping to speak with you to learn a bit more about your husband."

Nan Stewart frowned, but opened the door wider. "Of course. Though it seems odd that the FBI would be interested in a gator attack."

Camille nodded, understanding that this was a shared sentiment among most everyone else involved in the case. Nan led them through a foyer and into a hallway that led into a living room and a kitchen. Camille spotted two people in the living room, sitting quietly and watching TV at low volume. The entire house had the somber feeling of a home where someone had just died. She assumed the funeral was likely tomorrow or the next day.

Nan took them into the kitchen, but nodded back to the living room.

"My sisters," she said. "They've been staying with me ever since Earl died."

Camille could sense the woman's sadness behind her tired eyes. She seemed to be at the point of resigned acceptance, the sort of eerie calm that comes over spouses that have lost their partner—a calm that almost always broke and came flooding out as grief during the funeral and the days after.

"So what can I help you with?" she asked. She paced nervously in the kitchen, the counters behind her filled with foods brought in by loved ones in the wake of losing her husband.

"Well, there has been a second death that seems to also be an alligator attack," Camille said. "And whenever there are two or more deaths in a smaller community, the State Police will often call in the bureau. Even in this case, to make certain it was indeed gator attacks is a standard practice to make sure we don't need to open an active case."

Nan looked confused for a moment, her hands compulsively tearing back a corner of aluminum foil that was covering a plate and then pushing it back down. "Do you have reason to think Earl WASN'T killed by an alligator?"

"Not a strong reason, no," Palmer said. Camille wasn't upset that he answered so soon. It was really was the best reason, after all, and he was probably only trying to keep the woman calm. "But the scene where the most recent victim was found does have us looking a bit closer."

"That's right," Camille said. "So we're really here to just ask about Mr. Stewart. Do you know what he was up to on the day of the attack?"

"It was a Saturday, and when he left the house, he said he was going to the convenience store for some beer. And that was it. That was the last time I saw him alive."

The words were heavy, but she didn't cry. She simply stared out into nothing, as if willing the grief to fully return to her.

"Had he been acting out of sorts in any way recently?" Camille asked. "Was there anything new going on in his life?"

Nan laughed, bitterly. "There was always something new going on with Earl. He was always trying to find the next new thing to occupy his time. He tried the stock market, different books and movies. He was very quick to get interested in new things. He even tried taking up painting but God, he was awful at it. But in the last few days, he was acting more like himself than he had in a long time. He seemed content to just *be*. He was... happy."

"Happy?" Palmer asked. "In what way?"

"He was just... cheerful. He'd started talking about retirement even though it wouldn't be a possibility for another nine or ten years. He was talking about moving to the Keys. He kept saying he wanted to take me on a cruise, and he had us both eating mangoes for breakfast. He'd never said anything about retiring before and I thought he was just playing with my head. But he kept talking about how much he loved being with me and how he was so incredibly happy."

"Did he ever spend time out in the swamps?" Camille asked.

"Some. He fished every now and then...another of those things he was trying to use to make himself happy. But to my knowledge, he hadn't been out there in quite some time."

"Did Mr. Stewart have any close friends?"

"No. He was close to my family, but he didn't have any friends."

"Has there been anyone unusual in the neighborhood that you'd seen around your home?" Palmer asked.

"No." Nan seemed to be getting slightly worried at the direction the questions were going. She'd ripped the entire corner of aluminum foil off of the plate and had started rolling it up into a ball compulsively in her hands.

"Where did he work?" Camille asked.

"Out at Barlo Feed. They make and bag up dog food, cat food, and special farm-based feed. He'd been there for over twenty years."

"No enemies at work?" Camille said.

Again, Nan laughed in a dry and airless way. "Earl? No. Everyone loved that man. And I don't say that just because I'm his wife. He didn't have many friends but you can ask just about anyone in Hen Creek or surrounding towns. He was just the sort of man people got along with. I think that in our twenty-four years of marriage, I saw him angry a grand total of twice."

Camille and Palmer shared a glance, sensing that this was yet again gong to lead to nothing of real importance.

"Just one more thing, Mrs. Stewart," she said. "Were you and Mr. Stewart close with the Pullman family out of Hen Creek?"

"Pullman?" Nan thought about it for a moment and shook her head. "No. I don't believe that name rings a bell. That's just me, though. Earl may have known someone with that name but just in passing."

"Thank you," Camille said. "We'll leave you to your privacy now."

"Sorry for your loss," Palmer added in an obligatory way.

Nan walked them to the door and just as the agents stepped out onto her porch, Nan stopped them.

"Is...is everything okay?" she asked. "I'm sorry, but it does seem odd having FBI agents looking into deaths that are being called gator attacks."

"Yes ma'am," Camille said. "Everything is okay. Just checking off boxes as we can."

Nan nodded and waved them off as they headed out. But even as they got in the car and Camille looked at Nan Stewart through the windshield, standing on her porch, she could see the uncertainty in the widow's face.

CHAPTER TEN

He used his father's old gig to spear the frog just before it tried to leap away from him. He held the gig up for a moment, watching the toad flail and kick its back legs. Its eerie little eyes looked around frantically and then, like its legs, it went still.

He smiled. Dinner was served, and he'd always had a soft spot for frog legs. He knew many would frown upon it but when cooked just right, they could be delicious.

With his dinner still strung on the end of the gig, he walked back to the bank along the marsh and stepped into his little aluminum boat. The bottom of it was lined with old fishing line and dried fish guts. The oar he used to paddle away from the bank was stained with blood on the end, the result of dinner from two nights ago in the form of a slow groundhog.

He rowed the small boat through the weed-littered marsh, heading to the old houseboat that waited on the other side. The sound of his oar easing through the water was the only unnatural sound he could hear—probably the only unnatural sound around for at least two or three miles.

Frogs croaked, crickets chirped, and all manner of other animals began to call out and grow excited as the day began to cool and night inched its way along. The approach of night was something he could feel on the swamp a good three hours before the sun started to go down. He could read many different things about the swamps of Louisiana by just the way the air felt, the way the creatures of the forests behaved.

He pulled the little aluminum boat through a grove of cattails and unnamable weeds. As he came around a slight bend where the marsh gave way to a proper swamp, his houseboat came into better view.

It was old and the engine was basically shot, but it was all he needed. To him, it was home.

He'd been living on it for a month now. Out here in the middle of nothing, he felt like a god, silent and with his thoughts in all of the silence.

Out here, his mother could not scold him.

Out here, his father could not use the belt or, on his longer drunken nights, the old baseball bat.

This was his home now, and he was fine with that.

He docked the little boat by the side of the house boat and climbed aboard. He sat down on the back, above the useless engine compartment, and started to work on the frog with one of the three knives he kept at the ready.

The sun started to dip from its place in the sky when the frog was free of its carcass and skinned. He went to his cabin and got out a pot and some oil.

He put the pot on the stove and lit the burner, melted a few pieces of butter in the pan and threw in a few diced onions. While that was sizzling, he threw the frog in the pan.

He waited for the sizzling to die down and then poured in some more butter and a bit of salt. He started to toss the pieces of frog in the pan, letting them get a nice golden brown on each side.

He turned off the stove and went out to sit on the rear of the boat.

No one knew he was out here and even if they did, they couldn't find him. It was all for the better really. To quote his mother, there were "a lot of bad men out there."

He supposed he was one of those bad men now. He'd done things this week that he knew were wrong...but had felt right.

Out here, he wouldn't be found. No one came out here. It was one of the parts of the swamp most people had forgotten—a place alive with huge snakes, dangerous crocs, and herons and cranes more beautiful than any ever seen nearer the roads and cities.

Out here, the thought of getting caught never crossed his mind. He was one with this forgotten corner of nature and there were times, especially at night when the fireflies came out and created galaxies over the swamp, that he felt immortal.

In this new home, he supposed he *was* like a god. This was the place he had brought two people to be judged, to be tested.

And there would be a third soon.

He ate the frog legs and walked back inside to grab a beer. He didn't have a fridge on the boat, so he drank the Budweiser warm. And as he let the food settle and the beer go down as smooth as warm beer can, he thought of that third victim.

He thought of the next victim with a smile—a smile that dropped on the right side of his badly scarred face.

CHAPTER ELEVEN

Camille and Palmer made their way to the Hen Creek police department shortly after speaking with Nan Stewart. It was nearing three in the afternoon and Camille could tell that Palmer was having to take extra efforts not to complain too badly about how deep she was digging.

She understood it, really. Most other agents would have likely called it a day after seeing the bodies. But there were two things that stood out in her head that she was not willing to let go of. First, there was the absolutely lack of struggle or prints at the sites where the bodies had been found. Second, there was the bruise she'd seen on the back of Wendy Pullman's right leg. It was far too noticeable and, unless the gator had somehow punched her, looked out of place. She was very much aware that she was being a bit too picky, but something about it simply nagged at her.

She did sense, though, that she may only have a few more hours to try to find something. If she wasn't back in New Orleans by six or so with some sort of debrief for McCutcheon, she was going to probably get the riot act read to her.

As she and Palmer walked into the station, she wasn't quite sure what came next. In her mind, she removed the alligator factor from the case. She viewed it as a normal case, asking herself what her next step would be.

The answer was easy: the only source of leads they might have would be from Wendy Pullman's dating app. Her mother had said Wendy had been on a few dates recently as a result of the app. In a normal case, that would be a promising lead.

"I don't see Humphrey anywhere," Palmer said. There was some humor in his voice, maybe a bit of snark.

It was clear that Humphrey wasn't around because they could see the entire police station from where they stood just in front of the doors. It was a very small building consisting of a large, open space. A young, polished-looking man sat at the front desk and behind him, eight other desks were all positioned around one another. It looked more like a derelict call center than a police department. There were three officers at three of the desks but Humphrey wasn't one of them.

Camille walked up to the front desk and showed her badge and ID to the man.

"I'm Agent Camille Grace. My partner and I have been working with Deputy Humphrey on these gator cases. I was wondering if there might be a place we could temporarily set up?"

The man looked confused and maybe a little scared. "Not really. I mean, you can sit over there in the waiting area."

He pointed over to the right, where two chairs sat on either side of a large potted plant.

As they walked over to the waiting area, Palmer seemed less jovial than usual. Camille supposed he was quickly becoming very much done with a case that he truly didn't think was worth looking into.

"What are you thinking for next steps?" Palmer asked.

"I'm thinking I want a look at Wendy Pullman's dating app," she answered as she pulled out her cellphone. She navigated to the case files that were sent to the bureau just nine hours ago and located Sue Pullman's phone number. She was about to call it to see if Mrs. Pullman might know more about the dating app and who her daughter may have met on it when the front door opened.

Deputy Humphrey came in, walking behind a large and very angry-looking man.

Both men scanned the room, their eyes settling on the agents in the waiting area. The larger man came storming over with Humphrey beside him. The lead man was not only tall, but had shoulders that looked like they might be able to haul trees around. He had a thick beard that covered the lower half of what looked to be an older, handsome face. The nameplate above his breast read CPT. BEECHER.

Camille recalled speaking with him very briefly while sitting in McCutcheon's office.

"Agents Grace and Palmer?"

"That's us," Camille said.

Beecher stopped a few feet away and it was clear that he was doing his best to restrain himself. His jaw seemed clenched and he had made fists out of his hands.

"I'm told by the county coroner that you requested the body of Wendy Pullman to be moved. Why is that?"

"Because the paperwork was lazy and sloppy."

"In your opinion," Beecher said.

"With all due respect, did you see the reports?"

"I did not. But I assume it was done thoroughly."

"I highly suggest you take another look. I'm sorry, but if the county wants these deaths safely wrapped up as gator attacks, I can't very well give such a statement if I'm working with lackluster records and reports."

"Reports? Agent Grace...did you come down here hoping to arrest an alligator?"

Camille had to keep herself from smirking at the smart-ass comment. "No, I'm here because two people are dead, and the State Police asked us to come down to make sure there was no foul play...that it is indeed gators. But the more I see, the less convinced I am that it is so cut and dry. It's possible that there are gators involved, but I can tell you that the county is going to have to tighten its belt if you want this done right."

Beecher let out a long sigh and took a step back. He seemed to be weighing his words as his eyes darted back and forth. He was likely trying to decide exactly how to play the situation.

"Agent Grace, I want you to know that I am committed to finding out what happened here. I knew Wendy Pullman. I went to school with her father. But you can't come into town and turn this into a spectacle."

"All I did was request that a body be looked at by a second set of eyes."

"And when that second set of eyes ends up giving you the same results as our county coroner, will you be satisfied?"

"That's very likely."

Beecher nodded and looked back to Humphrey. "I'm sure you didn't help at all on this, did you?"

"I presented the facts as I saw them, sir," Humphrey said. "No gator tracks and the bodies found in locations that didn't quite line up with the gator narrative."

"Christ Almighty," Beecher said, his hands now on his hips. He turned back to the agents, clearly doing his best to seem as polite as he could while seething with anger.

"You're welcome to whatever resources you need, agents. But after you get your secondary results from your New Orleans coroner, I'd really love to not have an FBI presence around here."

"Likewise," Palmer said, nearly as irritated as Beecher seemed.

Beecher didn't say another word. He walked with that same speed and force out toward the desks in the back half of the building.

Humphrey came over to them, an apologetic look on his face.

"So, he's not very pleasant," Palmer said. Then, looking to Camille, he added: "I have to say I agree with some of what he said, though."

"You think I'm wasting our time?"

"I do. I'm sorry, but yes."

"Okay, so let's knock it out quick then," she said surprised at how quickly the wave of anger came upon her. "Deputy Humphrey, does the department have Wendy Pullman's phone?"

"No, ma'am. As far as I know, it's still with her mother. But we did get backups of her social media just in case."

Camille didn't quite understand this. It seemed like someone, maybe even just Humphrey, had thought the murders were suspect enough to warrant actual police work. But she also assumed that if Beecher knew such a measure was taken, he'd scoff at it.

"Social media?" she said. "Do you recall anything about a dating app?"

"Yeah, actually. I don't remember the name of it, though."

"Can you show me?"

"Yeah. Come on and I can show you now."

Camille followed Humphrey and she noticed that Palmer was slow to move. When he did get up from his chair and followed after them, she shook her head.

"It's clear you're not into this. I get it. So why don't we sort of divide and conquer? I'll look into this if you want to see what you can find about gator attacks over the last two years or so. See if there were any in the areas we're looking into."

"I can do that," he said without much enthusiasm.

"I can get you logged into the system in a second," Humphrey said. He seemed pleased to be the connecting point with the bureau as he sat down at his desk. He woke up his laptop, opened up a folder, clicked around for a bit, and then typed in a password.

"Help yourself," he told Camille, getting up from the chair. He then wandered off to show Palmer where he could start searching alligator attacks.

Camille felt very much out of place as she sat down in Humphrey's well-worn desk chair. She saw that he had pulled up the information that had been backed up from the dating app. Looking at it, she frowned. She understood how everyone (aside from Humphrey) was ready to call this an easy case...or not a case at all.

There were only six hits on the dating app logs. Of those six, only four had resulted in dates. The backups had the messages Wendy Pullman and her potential suitors had sent back and forth as well as a note as to whether or not Wendy had pursued them beyond initial conversations.

Camille took a moment to read over the information on the four men. At first, she saw nothing impressive. They all seemed to be men of about equal age, clean-cut guys that weren't spouting dirty talk right away. One was a banker from New Orleans, another was the co-owner of a construction company located in Houma.

When she read the bio on the third man, her jaw literally fell open. She read it again, making sure she'd read it right.

"How the hell did no one see this?" she said out loud.

The third man's name was Carl Griffin. He lived in a town she'd never heard of, Nobles, and his primary employment was listed as "dock repairs and boat maintenance."

But it was what he'd listed under *Other Interests and Hobbies* that really caught Camille's attention.

Alligator handling.

CHAPTER TWELVE

Before Camille allowed herself to jump to extreme conclusions, she flagged down Humphrey. He'd just finished getting Palmer set up on the station's network and when he came back over to his desk, he looked ecstatic to be such a help to the visiting agents.

"You find something already?" he asked.

"Maybe. Something worth looking into, anyway. You know of a town called Nobles?"

"Yeah. Not much bigger than Hen Creek, to tell you the truth. About a twenty-minute drive south of here."

"I was wondering if you could get me on the database, too. I'd like to look up one of these guys on Wendy Pullman's dating app to see if he has a record of any kind."

Humphrey gladly did so and had her logged into the station's criminal database within just a few seconds. Camille stood up to give Humphrey his chair, but waved the gesture off.

"Make yourself at home," he said. "I don't know how much longer you'll have free reign over everything. Beecher has been known to lose his cool pretty quickly."

"You mean what I saw back there wasn't him having already lost his cool?"

Humphrey shook his head and laughed. "No. Not even close."

He walked away, leaving Camille to look through the database. She typed in Carl Griffin's name, with the location of Noble, Louisiana.

She wasn't sure what to expect. On the one hand, she thought a man that dabbled in alligator handling would be the careful sort because...well, caution was surely something you needed to have in abundance for such an interest. On the other hand, there was without a doubt a degree off recklessness and irresponsibility there as well.

When his name came up, she saw that aside from two speeding tickets, the only other thing on his record was a note about his calling in to the police last year to complain about a financial issue without someone in the Hen Creek area. The report did not give any more details about the call, but there was an internal link to another page on the database. She clicked it, the page opened up, and she read for less than five seconds before she found herself chuckling.

"Are you freaking kidding me?" she said. She said it so loud that she attracted the attention of an officer sitting two desks away.

In May of last year, Carl Griffin had called the police to see if there was anything within the law that he could do to make sure a client that was dodging payment could be taken to court over a rather small amount.

The name of that client was Earl Stewart.

Does no one around here do their jobs? she wondered. She knew that attitudes had likely gotten lazy on these deaths because they were, at first glance, obvious gator attacks. But now that she considered it and had this binding link in her face, she started to think it would be a brilliant way for a killer to make sure their tracks were covered.

She used the database to get Carl Griffin's address and then got up from Humphrey's desk. She nearly started straight for the front doors but figured she should at least tell Palmer where she was headed. After all, she wasn't mad at him, but she knew if they didn't spend some time apart, it might come to that.

She found him at a small cubicle space all the way to the right, planted in front of a laptop screen.

"I've got a pretty good lead," she said. "I'm heading out to the town of Noble, about twenty minutes away, to look into a guy named Carl Griffin. There's a link between him and gators as well as both victims. Might be nothing, but seems far too coincidental to ignore."

He started to get up, but she shook her head. "No, it's okay. You stay here and finish this up. I'll be back."

"Camille, you don't have to be like that."

"I'm not being any sort of way. I'm being smart. Divide and conquer, and let's get out of here as soon as possible, right?"

Palmer shrugged and turned his attention back to the screen. After a few silent seconds, it was clear that this was the only response she was going to get.

Camille left him there and headed outside. It was getting later, the heat fading a bit as she got into the bureau sedan. She plugged Griffin's address into her GPS and headed off in search of what she hoped might finally lead to some sort of evidence that there were more than gators at play here.

***

Carl Griffin lived in a cute log cabin down a thin dirt road. The dirt road diverted off of a secondary road that seemed to spear itself between Hen Creek, Noble, and several other small towns that all looked the same—often not even having businesses within them, just a series of ramshackle houses and mobile homes.

Griffin's cabin was situated at the bottom of a small hill, the jungle-like wall of forest and swamplands stretching out behind his property. When she parked in his driveway and stepped out, Camille could smell the swamp in the air. Stagnant, something resembling the rot of an animal, dead on the side of the highway.

She noted that there was a newer model Ford pickup in the driveway as she made her way to front door of the cabin. Off to the right, all the way at the backside of the property, she saw what looked like a modified dog pen. It was made of slats of metal thicker than anything she'd ever seen in a dog pen.

Stepping up onto the porch, Camille knocked and got a cheerful response right away.

"Hold one sec, please!" came the response.

Camille waited, listening to someone shuffling toward the door. When the door was opened, a man of about thirty or so looked out at her.

Griffin looked to be a little over six feet tall. He had a shaved head that still looked somewhat greasy, and he wore a pair of baggy shorts that were in good condition. Only a pair of sandals adorned his feet, his bare chest and arms exposed.

He looked confused to find a stranger on his doorstep but then smiled when he realized the stranger was an attractive woman dressed rather nicely.

"Can I help you?" he asked.

"Yes," Camille said, taking out her badge. "I'm Special Agent Camille Grace, with the FBI. I'm working a case out of the Hen Creek area, investigating two recent deaths that look to be the result of alligator attacks."

"Oh my God, that's terrible."

Camille watched him carefully, gauging his body language and the expression of his eyes to try judging if the shock of it was real. "I do need to tell you that your name has come up as we've tried to make sure there was no foul play involved."

"My name? Why?"

"One of the victims is a woman named Wendy Pullman. Your name was pulled off of a dating app on her phone. And it was also noted that your Other Interests section stated that you were an alligator handler. So, you can see the connection, right?"

"Ah," he said, both sad and relieved at the same time. "I see, yes, of course. Yes, I am an alligator handler."

"And do you also know a man named Earl Stewart?"

"Earl, yeah, I knew him. And I heard the news, too. I was...wait. Are you insinuating I had something to do with their deaths?"

"I thought your link to the three cornerstones of this case was worth a trip out here. Now, can I come in and speak with you?"

She saw few a flicker of irritation cloud Griffin's vision as he tried to sort out what had transpired over the past thirty seconds or so.

"Actually, if you'll allow me, I'd like to speak with you outside. Out in the backyard, actually. I'd like to show you something."

She nearly rejected this suggestion but decided to let it roll. He wasn't denying anything and seemed willing to speak. He as didn't appear to be any threat.

"That's fine," she said. "But I'd really like to not drag this out."

"For sure," he said, stepping out onto the porch. When he started down the stairs, his lack of a shirt allowed her to see a long-healed scar along his back. It was about eight inches in length right across the bottom of his shoulder blade. It looked quite a bit like the bite marks she'd seen on Wendy Pullman and the picture of Earl Stewart.

Griffin led her to the back of the property, in the direction of the strange pens she'd spotted as she'd walked to his front door.

"What do you plan on showing me?" Camille asked as they made it halfway across his backyard. She still didn't feel as if she were in danger, but she *did* feel as if the forests were starting to press in all around them.

"The alligator pens," he said.

"You keep alligators on your property?"

"Yes. And before you ask, I do have permits."

"*Why* do you have alligators on your property?"

They approached the pen now—one large pen that was broken down into several smaller ones. The primary pen was circular in shape, made much like a dog pen but with stronger material. A small trench had been dug around the outside with rows of wire blocking it off. She assumed this was a secondary defense just in case a gator got out of the pen. Inside the pen, there were shallow pools of water; some were nothing more than holes in the ground while there were also a few plastic kiddie pools.

There was a small alligator in one of the pools, and another one pressed up against the far corner of the pen, as if trying to hide.

"I do this as sort of a second job," Griffin explained.

"Raising alligators?"

"Sort of. I train them. I'm sort of an entertainer. I work with them at fairs, birthday parties, special events and things like that."

"What sort of work?" Camille asked. Seeing the gators so close up and imagining one of them taking the meat off of Wendy Pullman's leg unnerved her. And though Griffin seemed to be fully transparent and oddly proud, the sight did not ease her suspicions about him.

"The small one in the pool right there...I can get him to actually roll over. He needs a snack right after, though, or he gets cranky. Now for the bigger one, his name is Zeus, I can stick my head in his mouth and he won't bite."

The idea seemed preposterous to her. She knew people did this sort of thing as circus acts and things of that nature, but to actually speak with someone that did it as if it were just another job was surreal.

"Did Wendy Pullman ever see these gators?"

"No. We never actually met. Just talked about it."

This was true. She'd tried setting a trap for him; she'd read all of the exchanges between the two of them in the logs.

"And what about Earl Stewart?"

She noted a change in Griffin's demeanor right away. He went from being the proud owner of two alligators that did his little tricks to a man that was becoming defensive about the sudden appearance of an FBI agent at his door.

"Earl Stewart owed me money for some dock work I did for him about two years ago. He never paid me a single cent. And after I called a few times and even gave him a face-to-face visit, he still never paid. So I called the police to see what steps I could take."

"And that was it?"

"The courts sent him some papers but I never heard anything else. And I need you to understand this...I know how screwy this seems. Me having the gators and all that's happened this week. But I don't appreciate the idea that you're here to accuse me of murder."

"I'm accusing you of nothing. But your link to both victims and your rather proud admission that you not only handle alligators but have two of them as pets makes you a very interesting suspect." She waited a beat before she dropped the next line, not sure how he was going to handle it. "Mr. Griffin, I need you to come with me, down to the station. Just to answer some questions on the record."

"Sorry. That's not going to happen."

"You're not under arrest. I just need you to cooperate with—"

"No. This is insane."

"I'll ask you again, Mr. Griffin. And if you refuse, I *will* have to arrest you."

"I'd like to see you try it, bitch."

So she showed him.

She reached out with her left hand at lightning speed, pushing him hard against the pen. The smaller gator in the pool thrashed a bit at the commotion. Camille kept her eyes on Griffin, knowing full well if her eyes locked on one of the gators, he could easily slip away.

She went for her cuffs, still moving fast, but Griffin managed to slip away from her, using the pen's fencing to pull away. As he did, he brought a right hand around, aimed for her face. She dodged it easily, not even having to step away. She caught his arm, bent over slightly, and tossed him to the ground.

She then fell horizontally on top of him, bringing his arm back behind him in a modified arm bar. She slapped the cuffs on him and was back on her feet in less than five seconds.

"There," she said. "I tried. Seems like I succeeded."

She reached down to haul him up to his feet. As she did, she noticed that the larger gator had moved forward. His snout was nearly at the fencing, peering out to her over the trench to see what was going on. It creeped her out more than she cared to admit.

As she walked Griffin back across his yard towards her car, she could swear she still felt those reptilian eyes on her.

CHAPTER THIRTEEN

Done with his digging into recent alligator attacks in the area over the last two years, Palmer felt lost at sea. He was now stranded in a small-town police department where a visiting State Police captain was lurking around, pissed at him. He had Humphrey as an ally, he supposed, but Humphrey was set out about his own business.

As he occupied himself with looking over the eight reports of gator attacks from the last two years, Palmer started to understand that he had not been the best impromptu partner today. First of all, he'd pretty much invited himself to tag along, and within just a few hours he'd started complaining that Camille was trying too hard to find something that was not there.

This was her first case under a new director. Of course she was going to want to make sure it was done to perfection. It was much easier to realize all of this while she was not there, while he sat in the strange police station without a friend or any real direction.

He still thought the most likely cause of these murders was gator attacks. He did understand where Camille was coming from, though. He just felt that she was stretching a bit. The reports he'd found while she'd been gone really didn't support either side of the coin. In the past two years, there had been eight alligator attacks in Hen Creek and the surrounding two counties. Of those eight, only one resulted in death. In three others there were grisly injuries, including one man losing his right arm from the elbow down. But in the other four reports, the victims had managed to escape without much damage. Of those four, the worst was a man that required twenty-five stitches in his left leg.

She'd been gone for about an hour now and while he wasn't really worried about her, he felt he should know where she was and how things were going. He thought about calling her but didn't want to come off as being overbearing.

With nothing better to do, he went back to the database, figuring he could look for unsolved murders where the bodies had been discovered in swampy areas. But just as he was about to log back in, the front doors to the station opened and Camille stepped in.

She wasn't alone. There was a man with her, shirtless and with his hands cuffed behind his back. There was a cut along the bottom of his chin, the blood trickling onto his bare chest.

Palmer got up right away. As he crossed the room, Humphrey also came rushing over.

"You okay?" Palmer asked Camille.

She only nodded, her attention already on Humphrey. "Deputy, where's the nearest interrogation room?"

In a slight state of shock, Humphrey waved her to follow him as he walked to the far right side of the building. He made his way past all of the desks and opened up one of three doors at the back. Palmer followed along behind her, taking note of the old, large scar on the man's back.

Palmer entered the room as Humphrey also walked inside, looking around nervously as if he wasn't sure what he should be doing. He closed the door when everyone was inside and stood motionlessly by it.

The interrogation room was old and poorly maintained. The walls were wood paneling, the cheap stuff that was likely no thicker than cardboard. The floor was old, scarred tile and the table that sat in the middle of the room looked like it might have once stood in a school cafeteria.

"This is Carl Griffin," Camille said as she led the man to one of the two chairs at the table. "His police records indicate that he had a bit of a financial hiccup with one of our victims, Earl Stewart. More recently, he started speaking with Wendy Pullman on a dating app. And to put some more icing on the cake, he has two alligators in pens on his property. He trains them."

"Oh my God," Humphrey said. He looked slightly embarrassed, as if he somehow knew someone at the Hen Creek PD had dropped the ball.

"I brought him in because when I pressed the least little bit, he became vocally aggressive. When I attempted to arrest him, he threw a punch."

"Not a smart move," Palmer said.

"No, no it wasn't. Now, Mr. Griffin, I need to know why you got so aggressive when I asked you to come in."

"Because I'm no killer. You think you're the first people to think I'm strange because of my work with gators?"

"The way you reacted to my questions lead me to believe you're very defensive about it," Camille said.

"And why shouldn't I be? I've been doing this for years and I've never had a problem. All of a sudden, there's a few dead people with gator bites taken out of them and I'm the main suspect? Yeah...it seems lazy as shit on your part and I felt singled out. I lost my temper and threw a punch."

"You threw a punch at a federal agent," Palmer said. "Even if you come off squeaky clean on this, that's a no-no."

"Look, I don't know what you want here. I told you," he said, looking directly at Camille. "Those gators are trained. They may nip at me from time to time, but they don't go for the kill."

"Mr. Griffin," Camille said, "can you provide proof of your whereabouts for the last week?"

Palmer watched as Griffin thought this over. When he saw the flicker of relief in the man's eyes, Palmer knew he was going to turn out to be innocent. It was more than simple relief he saw in the man's eyes. It was a look that seemed to say *Gotcha, bitch.*

"As a matter of fact, I can. Me and my gators were in Baton Rouge for three days, doing a little circuit there. Before that, we were in Panama City, Florida. I just got back yesterday evening." He seemed to read the defeat in the room. He grinned and went on. "I've got receipts from the trailer I rented to haul the gators, receipts for gas, pictures taken at the three events we participated in. So yeah...I can give you my whereabouts."

Palmer watched as Camille struggled to come up with another question. He wasn't all that familiar with her, sure, but this was the first time he'd ever seen her so flustered. Camille nodded curtly at Griffin and then turned for the door. Her eyes barely met Palmer's as she opened it and walked out.

Palmer regarded Humphrey with an apologetic frown. "Hold down the fort for a second, would you?"

He stepped out after Camille and saw her heading for the doors. He gave her some space but followed after her. She stepped outside and stood there for a moment, simply looking out across the lot. As Palmer approached the doors, she started pacing nervously.

Palmer stepped outside and when she turned to look at him, he saw the annoyance in her face.

"I know," she said. "I'm trying to find things that aren't there."

"Yeah, I think that might be true. But you also found a guy with clear links to both victims that has experience with handling and training alligators. That's a no-brainer. If you hadn't gone after him, I'd question your abilities as an agent."

She stopped pacing and leaned against the brick wall along the front of the building. "Maybe you're right. Maybe they're just gator attacks. Maybe I'm just...maybe I'm trying too hard."

"I think that might be true, too. But you know what? We've got to wait for the report from the coroner in New Orleans. Let's see what they have to say. Humphrey doesn't seem so sure, either, you know."

She gave him a look that he couldn't read clearly. She shook her head and said, "You don't need to pacify me."

"I'm not pacifying. It makes sense that some people in this area would *want* this to be gator attacks. It's easier to sell to the public than a rogue killer wandering around. This whole thing with Griffin and how perfect of a fit it seems...it helped me to understand how you're seeing it as something bigger. And because of that, maybe I'll stop being such an ass. Let's stick it out a bit longer and see what comes of it."

She chuckled. "Right now, it seems like the first thing will be to do some damage control in terms of Carl Griffin."

"He took a swing at you. He admitted it. I say we get him a shirt and let him stew in it for a bit."

"Sounds good to me. And Palmer...thanks. I know that once I get my mind focused on something, it can be hard to deter me."

"Yeah, I'm starting to learn that about you. Some might say it makes you a better agent."

"Why don't you go in there and tell that to Captain Beecher?"

"I might just do that," Palmer said. He turned back to the door and opened it for Camille. "Come on," he said. "Let's go find Mr. Griffin a shirt."

CHAPTER FOURTEEN

Gary Anderson walked across the parking lot of the Hornet's Nest, letting out a loud burp. He shuffled to his truck under the twin light-posts in the parking lot and unlocked his truck. His mind was on Lizzi, the hot little bartender he'd been trying to hook up with for about a year now. Truthfully, that's always where his mind was when he left the Hornet's Nest. Lizzi was one of a circulation of four bartenders and when she'd left early for the night, Gary decided he was done for the night, too.

Getting hammered on a Thursday night just wasn't as fun if Lizzi wasn't back behind the bar. She didn't have much up front but when she leaned over behind the bar to get something under a shelf and the black stripe of her thong showed, it was worth the average forty-dollar bar tab.

"One of these days, sweetie," he said into the night as he got behind the wheel. She'd been flirting with him for weeks now, a bit more than she doled out to the rest of the bar's patrons. They were the same age and though he didn't have much to offer, Gary knew that most women his age—just north of thirty—found him to be good looking.

In other words, he didn't think it was too unbelievable to think she might find him attractive. Certainly attractive enough to have a couple of one-night stands.

With that hope in mind, Gary cranked the engine of his old Chevy to life. As he flicked on his headlights and reached for the gearshift, he noticed the folded slip of paper tucked between his windshield wiper and the glass. Letting out another brutal belch, Gary opened the door and stepped out to retrieve it.

When he unfolded it, a simple note was waiting for him. He smiled as he read it.

9:30. Tent on the bank of the river at the end of Duggar's Trail. Better not be too drunk. You've waited long enough and I expect you to perform. - Lizzi

"Hell yeah," he said, stuffing the note into his pocket.

He then checked his watch and saw that it was 9:07. Lizzi had left the Hornet's Nest no longer than half an hour ago. Had she left in such a hurry *just* for him? He wasn't sure...but the idea of her in a tent in the dark woods, waiting for him, was too much to ignore.

He hurried back into his truck and, though Duggar's Trail was no more than fifteen minutes away, he spun gravel as he quickly left the parking lot.

Gary's mind was a blur as he drove, wondering if he'd actually pull this off. It was all so sudden. So unexpected, if he were being honest with himself. He'd been breaking down Lizzi for months. Telling himself that if he didn't get her soon, someone else certainly would. Not that it would have stopped him. Even if someone else had nabbed her unofficially, he would have kept going after her. She was just so damned hot, the sort of woman that made your thoughts a jumbled, horny mess with just a simple glance in her direction.

Through all of the flirting and passing of beer across the bar, she'd hinted at it, on more than one occasion and he'd dared to hope. And now here it was: a challenge. A command. A direct order. All in the form of a note tucked between his windshield wipers.

He could already feel the excitement building. It was hard to sit still, harder yet to even drive.

He came to Duggar's Trail, a thin dirt road used for hunting in the fall and winter months, and left pretty much alone for the rest of the year. The trail itself gave way to several other roads, but the only one that went all the way down to the river was the main Duggar's Trail route.

Gary tried to remain calm but knowing what was up ahead, he pushed down on his foot, pressing the gas harder. Clouds of dust kicked up around the truck as he sped through the night. He slowed as he came to the small iron gate on the side of the road—a gate that was never closed and had been there for many years, no longer in use. He drove past the gate and sure enough, he saw a small flicker of light off in the distance. It bobbed and weaved, like a flashlight beam wandering around.

He parked the truck and stepped out. The night smelled sweet, and a chorus of tree frogs and crickets greeted him. He walked through a small cluster of weeds and down a slight hill. There, he saw not only the bobbing light, but the shape of a small tent. The river gurgled and cooed on the other side of it. The light was coming from within the tent, beckoning him.

"Here I come, baby," he said, loud enough for her to hear.

He hurried to the tent, pretty sure the front of his pants were about to explode. Then, as he reached for the zipper along the front of the small tent, a strange thought occurred to him.

How had she known he'd leave in time to get here at 9:30?

And....where was her car? He hadn't seen it when he parked his truck just up the hill. She could have parked somewhere else but...

Inside, something shifted. It sounded like the soft sounds of blankets or sleeping bags. And though there were alarm bells ringing in his head, he had to check it out. Christ, he was already here and really, the reward would certainly be worth the risk.

"You ready for this?" he asked.

He pulled the tent zipper down and, for just a moment, was blinded by the flashlight.

"Hey..." was all he said.

And when his eyes adjusted, he did not see Lizzi. Instead, there was a man there, his shirt off...and he was covered in scars. It was a face he knew, a face he'd hated for so long, a face—

The man surged forward, slashing out with a knife. The blade caught the beam of the flashlight and the light danced along it at the same moment it sank deep into Gary's neck.

Gary Anderson gasped and tried to scream as he stumbled backwards, falling away from the tent. He knew he hit the ground but after that, he wasn't sure what happened. All he felt was a terrible, numbing pain as the man from the tent fell on his back and plunged the knife in deep.

Gary caught a quick glance of the river before the night seemed to come alive, a single, living wall of darkness that swallowed him up completely.

Only...no, there was something else there in the darkness. It was coming out of the water, low to the ground. It moved slowly, crawling on its belly like a large snake.

But it wasn't a snake. It was bigger, wider...deadlier.

When Gary realized what it really was, he tried again to cry out, but there was nothing. All he could do was hope to die before the white, gnashing teeth of the alligator sank into him.

CHAPTER FIFTEEN

Night had fallen and the only thing Camille had to be remotely happy about was the fact that the Carl Griffin link seemed to have made a few people on the local police force happy. Sometimes, she supposed, fate had a way of offering little rewards in the face of failure.

She and Palmer were sitting in the bureau sedan, parked in front of a little dive called Goldie's Chicken, eating a dinner that was surprisingly delicious. It was one of only two places to eat in Hen Creek and seemed to be a rather popular spot judging from the packed lot. They were sharing a six-piece meal with all the fixings and Camille thought the coleslaw might be the best she'd ever eaten.

"So here's a question," Palmer said as he tossed the remnants of a chicken leg back into the greasy box containing their dinner. "What are we supposed to do about a hotel? I'd imagine the closest one is damn near all the way back in New Orleans."

"Well, then, let's just go back home," Camille said. " If we need to come back out for something in the coming days, it's not too long of a drive."

She emptied off the last of the coleslaw. "Maybe you were right. Maybe I was just trying too hard."

"Maybe trying to impress McCutcheon?"

"Not really. Just...I know how much I'd beat myself up if we found out a few months from now that it wasn't just gator attacks."

"Ah, you're one of *those* agents," he said with a grin. "All joking aside, though, I sort of admire it. I can't recall the last time I worked with another agent that was so dedicated. It's sort of a breath of fresh air."

"But you still think it's gator attacks, and that's the end of it?"

He shrugged and opened his mouth to answer but before he could say anything, Camille's cell phone rang. She noted the New Orleans area code and answered right away. She didn't think it would be McCutcheon but a little spike of doubt came up all the same. What if her new director was calling to ask her why it was taking so long to verify a couple of alligator attacks?

"This is Agent Grace," she answered.

"Agent Grace, hello. This is Reggie Combs with the coroner's office. I had a look at this body you had moved to us from Hen Creek and thought you'd want an update."

"Yes, I would," she said, taking the phone away from her head and placing it on speaker phone so Palmer could hear. "Did you find anything?"

"Not really...but at the same time, just enough to make me understand why you might be hesitant to label it as a gator attack and then call it a day."

"Such as?"

"Well, she *was* attacked by a gator, no doubt about it. But I also found a puncture wound on her upper abdomen. At first glance, I almost overlooked it because it is very close to more bite marks. But it goes deeper, and at a bit of an angle."

"A stab wound?" Palmer asked.

"Looks very much like it. And then there's the bruise on the back of the leg that is still intact. There are signs of a hematoma which indicates the limb was hit quite hard with something solid. The bruising seems to indicate the blow would have been somewhere close to the time of the stabbing—if that's what it is—and the alligator attack."

"Is there any way to determine if the gator attack was postmortem?" Camille asked.

"Sadly, no. I'm going to go ahead and say the puncture to the abdomen *is* a stab wound. And if I'm right on that, it and the bites from the gator seem to have occurred quite close to one another in terms of timeline."

A very likely stab wound. A blow to the back of the leg. And here she was, about to throw the towel in and claim it had been only a gator attack. She looked to Palmer and saw the genuine shock and interest on his face.

"Mr. Combs, this is an immense help. Thank you."

"Of course. Good luck out there. I'm no agent or detective but based on what I'm seeing with this body...you're looking at a murder case. Not a gator attack."

They ended the call and Palmer reached into their dinner box, fishing out a biscuit. "Well, I'm not going to lie and say I have no problem admitting when I'm wrong. In fact, I loathe doing it. But I guess I was wrong here."

"Happens to the best of us," Camille said, pulling up a number on her cellphone.

"Who are you calling?"

"Deputy Humphrey. Looks like we may need to find a place to stay rather than heading back home after all."

***

The only hotel between Hen Creek and the outer rim of New Orleans came in the form of a surprisingly tidy placed called Newcomb's Motel. It looked like a small penitentiary from the outside, all stale brick tones and featureless windows. It sat fifteen miles outside of Hen Creek, the sort of place where they offered brochures of things to do forty-five minutes further out in New Orleans.

Camille found her room clean and efficient. The smell of very old, stale cigarette smoke hung in the air but an overwhelming scent of lemon cleaner nearly eliminated it. She showered, letting the heat and the sweat of the day melt away from her, and then cranked the AC up before getting into bed.

Unsurprisingly, she thought of alligators as she closed her eyes. She also thought of Carl Griffin, a man that had trained gators so well that he felt somewhat comfortable sticking his head in their mouths. There were parts of his personality that seemed to fit what they were looking for now that they had a coroner also stating that there was a very good chance the victims had been killed and *then* fed to gators.

Well...fed, or just dumped for gators to find?

She thought there was a huge difference there and it might very well be one of the most important questions remaining.

This thought stayed in her head as she drifted off to sleep. Somewhere in the sludge of sleep, she had a dream that brought to mind hazy images of her father, calling her his good, sweet girl. He was telling her that she had to stay away from the pig pens, had to make sure no one knew. Only in the dream, there were alligators in the pig pen and there were severed body parts in the mud. Body parts that she felt certain belonged to her sister, Nanette.

When her cellphone rang, yanking her out of the dream, her heart was racing like a rabbit in her chest. She slapped at it instinctively, her eyes and her mind not yet fully adjusted to the waking world.

"Hello?" she asked.

"Agent Grace," a voice said. Male, but not Palmer. Thin and quiet, like the words were being spoken through a tin can. "It's Deputy Humphrey."

"Oh," she said. She sat up and put on the beside lamp. She squinted hard from the glare. "What...what time is it?"

"It's 3:15. Look, I'm sorry to wake you but there's another body."

"Gators?"

"Yes, gators. Same thing as Wendy Pullman and Earl Stewart."

"Okay," she said, quickly coming awake. "Can you text me the location? Palmer and I will be there as soon as we can."

CHAPTER SIXTEEN

Camille did her best to take in the sight of what remained of Gary Anderson without having to quickly turn away. A large bite had been taken out of his neck and lower face. He'd died in mid-scream, his frozen, final expression one of horror. His right arm had also been butchered badly; it was little more than a mess of blood and muscle from the shoulder to the elbow.

Humphrey stood a few paces behind Camille and Palmer, patiently waiting. Another man stood behind him, an older gentleman that looked like he'd gotten lost in the woods.

"Agents?" Humphrey said. "This gentleman is Al Bauer. He's the one that found the body and called it in."

Grateful to have anything to look at other than the remains of the man that had been identified by the license in his wallet as Gary Anderson, Camille turned to the man.

"How'd you find him?" she asked.

Bauer was visibly shaken and could barely look at Camille and Palmer when he replied. "I was outside, letting my dogs in for the night," he explained. "I heard this God awful scream coming from the woods not too far from my house, right up there." He turned to the right and pointed up a tree-shrouded hill. A muddy bank and a shallow cover separated the area where they stood and the hill. Through the trees, Camille could make out a few glowing lights.

"That's when you called?" Palmer asked.

"Well, I left the house because I figured maybe someone was hurt. But I called the cops when I was on the way through the woods. The screams had stopped by then."

"Where exactly was the body when you found it?" Camille asked.

"On the bank. I think he was trying to get away from the gators and maybe almost made it."

"You're sure there were gators?"

"Yeah," Bauer said. "If you look down on the bank on the other side of the river closer to my house, you can see the tracks."

"Thank you, Mr. Bauer," Humphrey cut in. "We may need to talk to you some more but I think we've got this covered."

"Fine with me," Bauer said in a shaky tone. "My God, the sight was bad enough...but the sound of those screams was awful. I pray I never have to hear anything like that ever again."

Camille forced herself to look at the ravaged corpse of Gary Anderson one more time. It was a very recent death. The blood was still wet, and his skin still had some color to it, visible even under the pale moonlight. She felt a wave of guilt pass through her, ushered along by sorrow. The source of guilt was an easy one to identify: she felt it was partially her fault because she'd not yet figured this case out. And the sorrow…well, anytime she looked a recent death in the face, the feeling of loss was heavy, even if she had no idea who the victim was.

"Agent Humphrey," Palmer said. "We're going to need you to do a thorough search of the area."

"Will do," Humphrey replied. "I've got a few men combing the area as we speak."

"Three bodies now," Camille said. "Three gator attacks in less than a week. How common would you say that is, Deputy?"

Humphrey shook his head. "Not common at all."

Steeling herself, Camille hunkered down to her haunches. She looked at his throat (what was left of it, anyway) and then his chest and stomach. He was wearing a white t-shirt, so when she saw the slight gash in his left side, it came rather easily.

"Right there," she said, pointing. Using just her fingertips, she took the tail of his shirt and lifted it up. It was soaked from the water, heavy, and covered in blood.

With the shirt lifted, the wound to his left side was even easier to see.

"Shit," Palmer said.

"Shit indeed," Camille said, looking to the mark that was obviously a stab wound.

"He was stabbed and then the gators got him," Humphrey said. "I'm sure folks would scream after getting stabbed, but not the way Al Bauer was describing. But if someone was being manhandled by gators..."

The sound of Humphrey's phone buzzing in his pocket made the Deputy jump a bit. Camille got back to her feet as he answered his phone. She scanned the area, taking a few steps closer down by the river as she listened to his one side of the brief conversation.

She saw no gator tracks on the bank on their side, but she knew that might not mean much. There was foliage and all sorts of debris along the bank. She did see where Gary Anderson had attempted to crawl his way out of the river, his hand print almost perfectly outlined in the soft dirt. She could only assume that Al Bauer's traipsing through the woods may have scared the gators off, allowing Gary Anderson to come to a stop on the bank.

"Agents, we might have a break," Humphrey said as he pocketed his phone. "One of my guys found Gary's truck about half a mile away from here."

"We're in the middle of nowhere," Palmer said. "Where the hell would he have parked?"

"It's a little cutover dirt road that connects a lot of these river places. Duggar's Trail," Humphrey said. "You guys want to head on over there? I'll stay here with the body until the ambulance arrives. You'll just want to follow this road out, take the next right and then another right after that."

Camille realized she was heading to the driver's side of the sedan without even thinking about it. Growing up in Upping, she'd been around roads like these, little dirt trails that wound their way through old hunting fields and alongside defunct logging tracts. She'd smoked her first joint on roads like these, lost her virginity in the back of a Chevy Cavalier on roads like these.

The sedan didn't handle them well, though. Bumping along the rough terrain led them through a thin strip of field, the bottom of the car scraping a bit. The first turn took them through a thick grove of trees and then back out into another night-shrouded field.

Sure enough, after another three minutes or so of inching along the dirt tracks, they came to a pickup truck and a police cruiser.

Camille pulled the sedan in behind the cruiser, the car barely fitting between the truck and the tree line. She killed the engine, and she and Palmer stepped out. A single officer was on the scene, approaching them from the front-end of the truck.

"Y'all Agent Grace and Agent Palmer, right?" the older officer said. His badge read Bradford. He was an older guy, the sort that Camille assumed usually spent most of his time riding a desk as he waited for the last year or so before retirement.

"Yeah, that's us," Palmer said. He lightly slapped the back of the truck and said, "And we're sure this is Gary Anderson's?"

"Yeah, some of us know Gary a little too well. He's got a talent for drinking too much and still being able to drive. I ran the plates just to be sure and yeah, it's Gary's."

Camille reached for the driver's side door handle but Bradford spoke up, stopping her. "You're welcome to check it out, of course," he said. "But I think I found something down on the banks. Not quite sure what it is yet."

Camille nodded and, under the guidance of a flashlight Bradford was holding, they ventured past the truck and down to the bank. This one was a bit clearer than the one where Gary Anderson had stopped breathing. And almost right away, Camille noticed something strange.

To their left, the grass was pressed down in a nearly perfect square shape. Because the grass was about four or five inches tall all around them, it was easy to see.

"What do you make of that?" Bradford asked.

Camille and Palmer walked over to the indentation. Palmer dropped to his knees and looked to the grass. He ran some of the depressed grass through his fingers thoughtfully.

"This happened recently," he said. "The grass is still flexible, still sort of springy."

Camille looked to the back right corner of the shape in the grass. She ran her hands along the ground and felt a slight dip. Within that dip, there was a hole. Curious, she checked the back left corner as well and found the same thing.

"There was a tent here," he said.

"A tent?" Bradford asked.

"Yes. The pegs went here and over there," she said, pointing.

"And here and here," Palmer said, eyeing the front corners.

"So the question is…where is it now?" Camille asked.

"It's got to be the killer, right?" Palmer said. "For some reason, they put a tent here. And Gary Anderson came out here to join them."

"Makes sense," Camille said. "But even still...why the gators? And how did the killer know where the gators would be?"

"So I'm now leaning towards human killer," Palmer said, "and YOU'RE the one hung up on gators?"

Camille got to her feet and looked out to the black, silk ribbon of river passing by. "No, there's definitely a killer. But he's damn good with gators, too. It's..."

"It's fucking strange is what it is," Bradford said from behind him.

Camille didn't think truer words had ever been spoken. Looking back to the indentation of the tent, Camille said, "Palmer...you know the area better than I do. How hard do you think it would be for me to find an expert on gators?"

"You mean aside from our buddy Carl Griffin? No one. I can make some calls, though."

"Well, you know," Bradford said, "I don't know if the fella is a gator expert, but I do know someone that works at the community college in Chalmette that used to be a zoology professor in Mississippi. Good guy. I think the force used him once or twice when we had some stray coyotes out and about a few years back."

"Can you get me his number?" Camille asked.

"Sure can. Give me about five minutes, would ya? It's almost four in the morning. Most people aren't exactly awake."

Bradford went to his cruiser and made a call while Camille looked back and forth between the tent and the river.

"This tent hasn't been gone for long," Palmer pointed out. "It might be a trail worth checking on, you know?"

"Would you run with that while I speak to this zoologist?"

"Sure But...say what you want, you *are* hung up on the gator aspect now."

"Yeah, I think I might be."

"You've joined the party too late," Palmer joked. "I've so moved on from that."

The joke fell rather flat as they continued to check over the camping site. There were multiple mysteries piling up now and with gators at one end of it, Camille couldn't help but feel as if they'd be running in very deadly circles if the case wasn't solved within another twenty-four hours.

But if the killer had indeed set a tent up here recently, it meant they were likely still in the area. And that, at least, gave her some hope.

CHAPTER SEVENTEEN

By the time seven o' clock rolled around, Camille wasn't feeling bogged down by a lack of sleep any longer. Instead, she used the little surge of adrenaline from the scene of Gary Anderson's death to urge her on. Still, when she arrived at the coffee shop in Chalmette, she was a bit too eager to grab a cup of coffee. While waiting in line, a man came through the door and also stepped into line. It was the sort of awkward first-meeting moment that was broken by the social conventions of coffee lines and other patrons but when they came out of it, Camille found herself sitting at a table in the back of the coffee shop with the zoologist Officer Bradford had connected her with.

His name was Zack Hayes, a thirty-one-year-old that had lived his entire life in the greater New Orleans area. He had the type of calm and collected exterior that made Camille feel that he was probably very easy-going. More than that, within just a minute of sitting across from him and getting through introductions, she found it hard to see him as a zoologist. He had the sort of appearance that made her think of men in their early thirties that still attended concerts and shot-gunned beers in an attempt to keep their grasp on youth for as long they could.

"I appreciate you meeting with me so early and on such short notice," she said once introductions were out of the way.

"Oh, of course. Sadly, this is exciting for me."

"Not much going on in the world of zoology teachers?"

"No. And to be clear, I'm not a zoology teacher. I'm a biology teacher at the community college. But I did study zoology in college. And I help out at the New Orleans Zoo from time to time...medicine, physical therapy for some of the aquatic animals, things like that."

Camille also found it easy to listen to him. He spoke with an eager excitement, an energy that seemed to match his appearance. Short-cut but shaggy hair that rarely saw a comb from the looks of it, along with deep, dark brown eyes. He had the sort of five o' clock shadow on his face that seemed like it might somehow be there all the time.

"So, I need to show you some pictures. I was told by Officer Bradford that you're okay with the sight of gore, right?"

"I don't enjoy it, but I can handle it. He may have told you I've served as a liaison for coyote attacks and ideas about how to push gator populations further away from populated areas."

"That's good," she said. She opened up a few of the file photos on her phone, including two of Gary Anderson that had been emailed to her just fifteen minutes ago. "First look...what can you tell me about these pictures?"

Zack took the phone and though he did grimace at first, he handled it like a pro.

"Three different victims, yeah?"

"That's right. One is just as recent as four hours ago."

He nodded and, after a few seconds, set the phone down. "Well, they're definitely alligator attacks. And likely from an older male."

"How can you tell that much from these pictures?"

"The bite width. The width of the teeth. Older male alligators have much wider jaws and wider teeth than the juveniles."

"Any idea on the size?"

"Maybe twelve to fourteen feet. Maybe a bit more. That's just a guess, of course. I'm not an expert in alligators. I know just enough to impress really boring people at parties."

"I grew up in Louisiana, in another area where gators were spotted here and there," she said. "So I know a bit about them, too. Isn't it true that gators will often wrestle their prey around a bit, sometimes even dragging them to the water and causing them to drown?"

"Yeah, it happens here and there. But not all of the time. They only behave that way when their prey is putting up a fight." He hesitated here for a moment and then looked at the phone again. "These three victims...how far apart are they?"

"Less than a week."

"Each?"

"No. I mean that all three were killed in the past week."

Zack scratched at his beard and then sipped from his coffee. Finally, he said, "I'll never claim something is impossible, but that is highly unlikely. Are they all locals?"

"They all lived within twenty miles of one another."

"Okay, we're inching closer to impossible."

"Why is that?"

"Well, because the national average for alligator-related deaths in the US is around three per year. So to get three in a single week in the same area...that's not going to happen."

"That's what I keep hearing." She hesitated here, and as she thought, Zack watched her closely. When their eyes met, he only smiled and held contact.

"Something wrong?" he asked.

"No. But you said gators tend to only drown their victims if they sense a fight in them, right?"

"Most of the time, yes."

"So let's say someone tossed, for example, a badly injured deer onto a river bank. How would a passing gator react?"

"There's no way to know for sure. I think in most cases, gators might think like we do...it's hard to pass up a free meal. Also, think of it like a shark; if there's blood in the water, it's usually frenzy time."

"During this case, we met with a man that trains alligators and uses them as props in little carny shows."

"Let me guess. Sticking his head in their mouths. That sort of thing?"

"That sort of thing, exactly."

"Yeah, that's the result of lots of tranquilizers and really rigid cause-and-effect training."

"Would you say it's easy to do?"

Zack laughed and shook his head. "God, no. You need to be both patient and pretty stupid." He sighed and leaned forward a bit. When their eyes met, Camille felt a quick flash of heat pass through her. "I'm not an FBI agent and would make a terrible cop," he said. "But in my uneducated opinion, I think the gators are secondary here."

"Meaning?" she asked, though she thought she already knew. Even a zoologist could see the facts of this case pretty clearly.

"I think you've got someone killing folks and trying to place the blame on alligators."

Camille smiled, a smile that felt maybe a bit too coquettish for her. "Maybe you'd make a good cop after all."

He shrugged. "Did I help?" he asked.

"You did. You've confirmed something that may help clear a path to closing the case, I think."

"Good. And you know, there might be something else you can look into. I don't know if it's related but it seems like something you'd want to check out. There's a nature preserve not too far away from the Hen Creek area, sort of out in the middle of nowhere. Gators aren't something they're known for; it's mostly swamp-area birds like herons, egrets, that sort of thing. But there *are* gators there. It's beautiful land, maybe just a little thick and off the beaten path for most people. But about five or six months ago, there were two guests to the reserve that disappeared."

"Were they ever found?"

"Not to my knowledge. Because it was a nature reserve, I worked with the federal government, not local PD. So honestly I don't even know how much the police in that area would even know about it."

"And why did they call on your services?"

"Just trying to figure out if there were any animals there that would serve as a threat to people that might get lost. Of course, gators were high on that list. But again, like I said, the bodies were simply never found. Not while I was involved with assisting, that is. Might be worth checking into."

"Absolutely. That's a promising lead. Maybe you *should* think about a career in law enforcement."

"Nah," he said with a smile. "Too stuffy. So…tell me, Agent Grace. I don't suppose you have the time during this case to sit with a boring zoologist and finish your coffee, do you?"

"Sorry to say I don't." And the way he looked at her made the comment quite true.

His disappointment sounded genuine, and she felt that heat again. Were they flirting and not even aware of it? Camille had always been a little slow to notice things like that. "Well, if you ever need the talents of a would-be zoologist again," he said. "Give me a call." Then, again looking directly into her eyes, he added: "You've got my number. And if you get a chance, maybe thank Bradford for me."

"I'll do that," she said.

It was harder than it should have been to get up from the table, but she finally managed. And when she got back into her car, she realized that she'd not only gotten confirmation of her original theory from Zack Hayes, but she may have also gotten a date or two out of the meeting as well.

And, more importantly, a bit more insight to carry back to Palmer and the case.

CHAPTER EIGHTEEN

When she arrived back at the station, Camille found Palmer in the station's only conference room. It was small and smelled of coffee and slight mildew. When she entered the room, Palmer was standing at the far wall, scribbling details down on a white board with Deputy Humphrey, Officer Bradford, and another officer named Swanson.

Camille paused as she stepped through the door, looking to the intricate little notes and connecting lines on the white board.

"Agent Grace," Palmer said with an excited grin. "Nice of you to join us!" He tossed his dry-erase marker at her and said, "Care to add what you've learned?"

She tossed the marker right back and shrugged. "Nothing to put up there. What I *can* tell you, though, is a zoologist that has more than a simple passing interest in alligators came to the same conclusion we're all currently on. And he was able to do it in about ten seconds without much leading by me."

"Can we have that conclusion spelled out?" Bradford asked.

Palmer beat Camille to it. "A killer that is doing his very best to make it appear as if it is gators killing his victims so we won't look in his direction."

"The hell of it," Humphrey said, "is that murders around here are about as uncommon as gator attacks."

Camille took the seat between Humphrey and Swanson. She looked over to Bradford, briefly grinning at Zack Hayes's comment about thanking him.

"So what's all this?" she asked, nodding to Palmer's notes on the whiteboard.

"This is us trying to make a connection between the three victims. One of the bits of vital information we came across while you were speaking to the zoologist was a note we found in Gary Anderson's pocket."

Humphrey took a sheet of paper out of the folder that sat in front of him and slid it over to her. There was a photocopy of the note on the paper.

9:30. Tent on the bank of the river at the end of Duggar's Trail. Better not be too drunk. You've waited long enough and I expect you to perform. - Lizzi

"Who is Lizzi?" she asked.

Palmer tapped at the same name up on the board. "The fellas here seem to think it's Lizzi Stone, a bartender at a place called the Hornet's Nest. You and I should probably pay her a visit quite soon."

"Any direct connection to the victims?" Camille asked.

"None that we know of," Bradford said.

"Nothing obvious, anyway," Humphrey added.

"What do we know about her?"

"Not a lot," Humphrey answered. "Her record is clean. I mean, she's that hot bartender that becomes the stuff of legend in small towns, you know? Other than that...there's nothing."

"So we now have three victims and still no clear connections?"

"But there *has* to be, right?" Swanson asked. "There has to be a connection between them."

"Three's not a lot to go on, though," Bradford said.

Humphrey shook his head. "In a town this size, that's just not true."

"Okay," Camille said. "So screw a connection between them. Maybe there isn't one. What if we look at each of them distinctly? Is there anything about these three people that would piss someone off?"

"A-ha," Palmer said, again tapping at his notes. Apparently, he was quite proud of them. "Let's have a look at that, shall we. The first victim was Earl Stewart. While a good enough guy overall, he seemed to be a real shit when it came to paying people for work on time. It may seem logical to some, but if you get on the bad side of that, he could be seen as a bully, right?"

"Sure," Camille said.

"Then with Wendy Pullman, it's sort of the same thing. She was rejecting dates on that dating app. We know that for sure. But who is to say she wasn't just as picky in real life? Say no to the wrong dude and you could be put on a hit list of sorts."

"Okay. And what about Gary Anderson?" Camille asked.

"Well, I hate to speak ill of the dead," Swanson said, "but he was a drunk asshole. About half the county would tell you the same thing."

"So why would Lizzi want him to meet her in private?" Bradford asked.

"Exactly," Camille said. "If she's the smoking hot bartender you guys claim her to be, I'm willing to bet anything she *didn't* ask him. I think someone lured him out with it."

"Someone that sat a tent up out on the banks close to where we found him gnawed on by a gator," Palmer added.

"Still, I think it's important we speak with Lizzi," Humphrey said. "If she was working last night, I think there's a good chance she might have seen him when he left."

Palmer nodded and this time tossed the marker to Humphrey. "That's step one for sure," he said. "You guys mind digging deeper into our three victims while we go have a talk with Lizzi Stone?"

"Sure," Humphrey said. "And what about Captain Beecher? Are we presenting this as a serial killer trying to feed his victims to gators?"

"That's what it is, so yes," Camille said.

Palmer frowned as he headed for the door and said, "But maybe try to make it sound a little less crazy than that."

“Also, Mr. Hayes, the zoologist, said there was a case he helped the government with a few months back—disappearances at a nature reserve somewhere nearby. I need some intel on that, as well.”

“Yeah, I can look into that,” Swanson said.

They all seemed eager to help, determination in their eyes. It was enough to send Camille out on their next errand with an extra bit of encouragement and drive, daring to hope this case would be closed before another day passed by.

***

One of the charms of working a case in a small town was that it took virtually no time to find an address for someone. It took less than twenty minutes to not only obtain Lizzi Stone's address but to also drive to her house from the police station.

Lizzi lived in a large model mobile home, the sort that didn't really look like a mobile home at all until you got closer to it. She'd decorated her porch to look cute, adorned with hanging plants and two lawn chairs siting on either side of a quaint patio table.

Camille knocked on the door, realizing that it was just after eight in the morning. And if Lizzi had indeed pulled a shift at the Hornet’s Nest the night before, she might still be asleep. She raised her hand to knock again but heard footsteps on the other side, followed by a surprisingly cheerful voice.

"Hold up! Coming!"

The door opened and a cute brunette with a hair bun came into view. She was wearing nothing but a long t-shirt and panties. She looked at Camille and said, "Can I help you?"

"Hi," Camille said, craning her neck to see inside the trailer. She could see a couch and a TV. "Sorry to bother you so early. I'm Agent Camille Grace and this is my partner Special Agent Palmer. Is now a good time to talk to you?"

"Agents? Like...with the FBI?"

"Yes."

Lizzi seemed to notice Palmer for the first time but showed no embarrassment or regret for what she was wearing. If Camille had the sort of body Lizzi had, she probably wouldn't either, though.

"Did I...I mean, am I in trouble?" she asked. And then, before Camille could answer, Lizzi said, "Ah hell, did something happen at the bar last night?"

"Not exactly, no," Camille said. "We do need to speak with you, though."

Lizzi looked very nervous as she nodded and opened the door wider. "Sure. Come on in. I just put the coffee on if you'd like some."

Camille stayed in the lead, noticing that Palmer was doing all he could not to look at Lizzi for too long. And even now that they were in her house, Lizzi made no attempts to further cover herself.

They entered into the living room. The sofa was littered with clothes and a laptop. The coffee table contained a few empty beer bottles and a cellphone.

"Lizzi, how well do you know a man named Gary Anderson?"

Lizzi was in the adjoined kitchen, getting down a mug. "Well enough, I guess. He's a regular down at the bar. Maybe too regular."

"Was there ever any sort of romantic relationship between the two of you?"

Lizzi wrinkled up her nose and shook her head. "God, no. Why? What's he been saying?"

Palmer spoke up now, his eyes doing their best to stay above Lizzi's shoulders. "Gary was found dead last night. We suspect it was murder."

"Oh my God! What...I mean, what happened?"

"We'd rather not share those details just yet," Camille said. "But what we *can* tell you is that a letter was in his pocket. It was letter written to Gary, from you, asking him to meet you out in a tent in the woods at 9:30."

The look of abject confusion and terror on Lizzi's face made her appear about five years younger, little more than a scared young girl.

"I swear to you...I have never, not a single time, written him any sort of note. Especially not one that might make him think I wanted him like that."

Camille didn't think the woman was putting on an act. She looked legitimately surprised at the turn of events. Her voice was squeaky with panic and her eyes were filled with worry rather than fear of being caught. Sadly, Camille had learned to tell the difference over the years.

"Did he ever come on to you?" Camille asked.

"Yeah, all the time."

"Aggressively?" Palmer asked.

"Maybe every now and then. But I don't think I ever gave him the impression that I was interested."

"I'll level with you here," Camille said. "There are certain factors about what we know so far that lead us to believe you very well didn't write the letter. However, all it will take is a simple handwriting analysis and checking your alibi to make sure. So...if there's anything at all you need to admit to, now is the time."

Lizzi shook her head vehemently. "I swear. No. I did not write any letter like that."

"Was there anyone that might know that he would jump at the opportunity to sleep with you?" Palmer asked.

"At the risk of sounding conceited, damn near every other person that ever saw him at the bar." She was pouring her coffee now and Camille noted a slight tremble to her arm.

"Can you tell us where you were last night?" Camille asked.

"Sure. I left the bar around 8:30. I was on the schedule to work until eleven, but it was slow, so I cut out early. After that, I went to a friend's house."

"They live around here?" Palmer asked.

"Yeah. Her name is Amy Sherman."

"And what did the two of you do?" Camille asked.

"Just hung out. Drank some cheap wine, watched some stuff on Netflix and then I came home. I was home by...two maybe? I didn't get to bed until around two-thirty."

"Did anyone else see you with her?"

"Yeah, her folks. She still lives with her parents. Her folks saw me for a bit but I don't think I saw them after like ten or so."

"Do you own a tent?" Camille asked.

"No. The idea of sleeping outside freaks me out. It's sort of gross, if you ask me."

Camille could tell the questioning was coming to an end. She'd likely have one of the local police check the alibi just to be official, but Camille believed her.

"Just one more thing," she said. "In all your time seeing Gary Anderson at the bar, was he ever in any fights? Was he ever trying to cause trouble?"

"Yeah, a few times. Usually when there was a football game on. But it never got really serious. There have been actual fights here and there at the bar but as far as I know, Gary was never in them. He did like to run his mouth, though. Always talking down to people. But it was Gary...so no one ever took it seriously."

Camille nodded and as she turned back for the door she again saw Palmer doing his best to keep his eyes from straying. In an odd yet simple way, he earned a bit more of her respect in that moment.

"Thank you, Ms. Stone." She reached into the inner pocket of her jacket and produced a business card. "If you do happen to think of anything else about Gary's behavior at the bar that might be sketchy, please call me."

"Sure." Lizzi eyed the card and seemed to go blank for a moment, as if the weight of what this all meant settled on her for the first time.

Outside, heading back for the car, Camille reached over and gave Palmer a gentle shove. "You're a man of great restraint, Palmer. Even I was having trouble keeping my eyes on task."

"I have no idea what you mean."

She chuckled and said, "Ah, but you're a terrible liar."

"So I've been told."

The light-heartedness wore off as they pulled out of Lizzi's driveway. They had three victims and a possible connection with bullying or threatening behavior, but nothing felt concrete. And at the center of it all were the damned gators, as of daring them to get closer, just a bit closer so they could sink their teeth in.

"Do you mind seeing if you can pull up the directions to the nature reserve?" she asked. "May as well strike while the iron's hot, right?"

"I'm not sure this iron is hot at all just yet," Palmer said, "but yes, I can do that."

The directions he pulled up indicated that the Eastman Nature Reserve was just eighteen miles away, winding them deeper into the woodlands around Hen Creek. The deeper they went, the closer

Camille felt to her past even though Upping was nearly a three-hour drive from where they were headed. She supposed it was the trees and the winding roads, leading into areas of the forest that seemed like they might reach down and choke the life out of her at any moment.

And when dealing with a case concerning alligators, it wasn't a great feeling.

CHAPTER NINETEEN

Camille thought the Eastman Nature Reserve looked like a poor man's Everglades. At first glance, it consisted of nothing more than a thin, two lane road that crept up to a small security gate. When she flashed her badge at the man in the security cabin, he seemed confused.

"Who are you her to speak to?" the man asked.

"Anyone in charge," Camille said. "Can you point us to anyone in particular?"

Still looking a little off his game, the guard finally gave an answer. "That'll be Ginny Nettle. You'll find her in the office attached to the visitor's center. About another mile and a half down this road."

He nodded to them as he pushed a button that lifted the old, iron rail that served as a gate across the road. As Camille drove the car through, Palmer looked into the rearview.

"He looked spooked. You think he's calling this Ginny Nettle to let her know the feds are here?"

"Yeah, I think that's likely."

The road wound through the surprisingly beautiful stretch of jungle-like forest. The trees that covered most of the area seemed to be designed to filter out a portion of the sun's light as much as possible, while providing ample shade and nutrient rich soil to the life forms that made their home there. It created a world of shadow and lush greenery that was both inviting but a little alarming all at once.

They drove on until the visitor's center came into view. It came out of nowhere and didn't look like anything special, just a small, cinderblock building with a small parking lot sitting in front of it. Two cars sat in the spaces furthest away from the building. A small secondary building sat off to the side of the visitor's center. As they parked, a woman came out of the door and waved at them.

"Looks like the guard *did* call her," Palmer noted as he reached for his door handle.

The woman, presumably the aforementioned Ginny Nettle, stood her ground but extended her hand as Camille and Palmer approached. She looked to be about fifty or so, her hair permed and her lipstick a bit overly pink. She wore casual attire—a floral shirt and basic slacks.

"Agents," she said. Camille shook her hand and introduced herself. "Agent Camille Grace, FBI."

"And Agent Palmer," Planet chimed in.

"Yes, Chester at the gate told me we had some federal guests. I'm Ginny Nettle. Is there anything I can do for you?"

"Well, we'd love to come inside and ask you a few questions," Camille said.

"About what, might I ask?" Her tone remained warm, but there was a hint of irritation to it now as well.

"I'd rather discuss it inside," Camille said.

"Sure, sure," Ginny said. She opened the door, allowing Camille and Palmer to enter first.

The building was mostly taken up by the room they walked into. The only break to it was a small hallway to the right that seemed to lead to only two other doors. Ginny's desk sat in a back corner of the room, a large and garish thing that looked as if it was polished once a day. When Ginny sat behind it, she kept her eyes locked on Camille and Palmer.

"So...what is this about?" she asked.

"We're working a case down in Hen Creek," Camille said. "It's a case connected with alligator attacks and we're trying to get a better understanding of what gator attacks look like around here."

"Ah, well, I'm afraid I can't help you with that. We've never had a gator attack on the reserve. More than that, I don't even know the last time a gator was spotted here. Maybe a month or two ago. They seem to come and go. I don't believe there's much for them to eat here, you see."

"Well, we're more interested in the two guests that disappeared a few months back. I believe the government was called in. What can you tell me about that?"

A brief flash of worry crossed Ginny's face. She apparently realized it was there because rather than simply pretending it had never appeared, she seemed to sink into it. A frown touched the corners of her too-pink lips.

"Well, there's not much to tell. There was nothing to be done about it. The wife of one of the missing came to the visitor's center, frantic, saying her husband was missing. The police sent out the search party, but the investigation fizzled out quickly. I can't say I was surprised."

"And why is that?"

"Well, the impression I got was that there was an argument between them. The State Police believed it, too. They assume the man escaped...that he simply left when the wife visited the restroom facilities." She sighed here and then, a bit too condescending in Camille's opinion, she added: "Really, all of this is in the official State Police report. Have you not seen a copy?"

Palmer apparently knew that Camille was about to blow a gasket because he was quick to keep the conversation going. "And what about the second disappearance? What can you tell us about that?"

"Well, I believe that happened about three weeks later."

"It was the same story as far as I know. Identical, at least at the start. A man went missing on one of the primary trails that cuts through the reserve. The wife was distraught. But this time the investigation didn't really make sense to me. I mean, it did at first: they found his car parked along the shoulder of the interstate. His wallet, money, credit cards and everything else was still there. They figured he had gotten confused, got in his car, and driven away."

"And that's it?" Palmer asked.

"That's the last I heard, yes. I don't mean to sound argumentative, but the State Police don't make a habit of filling me in on things just because they are vaguely linked to the reserve."

"Two people disappear on a nature reserve you manage, and you don't bother to follow up?" Camille asked.

"No, actually. It's not exactly the best press, as I'm sure you can imagine."

"You don't know anything else about what happened?" Camille asked.

Ginny's mouth hung open. A second later it snapped shut and her eyes settled on Camille. "What exactly are you implying?" Ginny asked.

"Nothing. I'm just wondering if you know anything else that could be relevant to our investigation. You must have had your own theories. You have to have wondered."

"What I do know is that none of it was gator related. And that seems to be what you're after, right?" Ginny leaned forward and made a point to look both of them in the eyes. "If you think those disappearances have something to do with your case on alligator attacks, you're barking up the wrong tree."

"Three people are dead in the Hen Creek area," Camille said. "We believe a killer is staging it to look like gator attacks. So yes...disappearances where there are known to be gators, no matter how few, seems to be quite relevant."

Ginny leaned back to her normal position, as if she had proven a point and already won the argument. "I've told you everything I know. If you need more, you'll just have to get your hands on copies of the police reports...which I do not have. So, is there anything else I can help you with?"

"No, not for now," Palmer said. "But if we do indeed find something worth digging into in those police reports, you can expect to see us again."

Ginny Nettle had nothing to say to that. She only smiled wanly and said, "Have a good day, agents."

Camille was a little uncomfortable with just how badly she wanted to smack the woman. The feeling was still on her like a cloud when she and Palmer got back outside.

"You think she's hiding something?" Camille asked as they got back into the car.

"Honestly, no. I think she's worried sick that those disappearances could cause some trouble to her privately owned nature reserve. I get it, I guess. But she was being a real bitch about it."

"I think I want to see those reports," Camille said. "I'll see if I can drum them up back at the station."

"Okay...so what next? Because I'm out of ideas."

"Same here," she said. And admitting it felt just as bad as not being able to slap Ginny Nettles.

"Well let's reconnect with Humphrey, then," Palmer said. "Maybe they've come up with something in their digging on the victims."

It was better than nothing, so Camille agreed with it. She guided the car back down the road. When they reached the guard shack and were allowed out, she could have sworn the guard smiled rather menacingly at them. With the trees crowded on all sides like lighthouses to her past, Camille sped more than was necessary down the reserve road and did not let up until they were back on the main highway.

CHAPTER TWENTY

As he carefully stepped down from the houseboat to the aluminum row boat docked at the side, he scanned the water. He knew how cunning and crafty alligators could be. One moment there would be only still, murky water and the next there would be a pair of reptilian eyes peering up just over the surface.

But the water was empty of them now. Off to his left a fish jumped and made a splash, and he could see a bullfrog bobbing up and down over on the bank closest to him. But no gators.

He rowed to the bank that would take him to the hidden clearing where he kept his truck parked. Gnats whirled overhead, stirred awake by the growing heat of the morning sun.

He knew who he would strike next. He also knew that he was getting too cocky. Killing Gary Anderson had been far too easy, too simple. He regretted luring him out to the river with a note; now, in the sun of a new day, he realized how it could come back to bite him.

He snickered at the choice of words as he continued to scan the water for any signs of gators.

He had a strained relationship with alligators. He respected them and often found himself in awe of them. Holdovers from the dinosaurs according to some, there was almost something mystical about them.

Yet at the same time, he feared them. And he had reason to. The scars on his back and along the side of his face, as well as the missing pinky on his left hand were reminders of how dangerous they could be. The moment from his youth where a gator had nearly killed him was never too far away from the center of his mind. And it came flooding back at maximum strength nearly every time he paddled his little boat over to the bank.

He had been just twelve years old, and it had been a hot summer day. He had been following some egrets, hoping to catch one. Not even a mile away from home, balancing along the banks, giggling whenever he'd lose balance and nearly fall into the waters of the swamps that sat eerily close to where his houseboat was currently anchored.

He'd come out to the woods to escape his brother's fists, a brother that had once caused him to pee his pants on the playground. A brother that had bloodied his nose three different times. A brother that was always on the hunt for him whenever their father wasn't showing enough love and attention.

His mind had been on this bully of a brother when the gator had come up out of nowhere and for about two or three seconds, he was convinced it was a demon, a demon straight out of hell that was trying to eat him alive.

He'd managed to escape its jaws mid-bite, his back a wall of knotted fire, his left pinky a painful and wailing memory in the belly of the beast. He'd climbed an old cypress tree, his blood trailing along its base. He'd screamed for twenty minutes or so before someone showed up. It had been his brother…the same one that had sent him running.

And then his brother had run away without helping. More help came ten minutes later and rescued him, beating the gator away with a fallen branch.

He shook the memory away as he came to the bank. With the memory came a little flicker of pain and an almost electric tingle down the center of his back, where most of the skin had been peeled away twenty years ago.

He stepped out of the boat and moored it to the same spindly oak he'd been using these past few weeks. The ground was soft, and he slipped as he hopped out of the boat, but he quickly regained his footing.

He made his way through the underbrush and came to his truck ten minutes later. He backed out of his hiding spot and came out on an old logging road that caused his shocks to groan, the frame of his truck bouncing and complaining the entire way.

He was almost done, he thought. When he'd started, he had four people he'd intended to get.

Three were already dead.

There was just one more left. And it might be a bit more difficult to lure them out. He'd saved this one for last on purpose, though.

One more...one more and he'd get the hell out of here. Out of this town, out of this state. He'd been doing some research and was pretty sure he'd be perfectly content living in Juarez, Mexico. He'd even emailed a real estate company down there and had some interest in a rundown bungalow.

But first, he had to finish what he'd started.

He directed his truck down a series of back roads, across the central road that ran through Hen Creek and then down more back roads.

He drove by the house of his next victim. They weren't home, but that was nothing new. But just seeing the house spurred him on, gave him the energy and drive to finish it off.

His hands shook with anticipation and nervous energy.

One more person. One more victim to feed to the gators and then he'd be gone.

Right now, he felt like those peering, reptilian eyes looking over the surface of the water. And when this was all over, he'd submerge into the muck and no one would be the wiser.

CHAPTER TWENTY ONE

Camille could tell by the defeated expression on Humphrey's face that he and his team hadn't had much luck with their attempts at digging through records. Camille and Palmer found Humphrey and Bradford sitting in the small conference room at the Hen Creek station, both leafing through files like men looking for a needle in a haystack.

"Any luck with Lizzi Stone?" Bradford asked.

"None," Palmer said as he and Camille joined them at the table.

"How about you guys?" Camille asked. "Anything at all? Even a nibble?"

Both men shook their heads. "Other than the fact they all lived within twenty-five miles of each other, there's absolutely nothing that links them."

"That's why I'm thinking the connection we're looking for might not even be among the victims," Camille said. "That is, maybe there's no thread between the three of them, but individual threads that connect each of them *to the killer*."

"Like maybe something personal?" Bradford said.

"Maybe."

"We know that Earl Stewart was sort of hardnosed when it came to business practices, for example," Palmer said. "So maybe they—,"

"But we can't find anything that connects them," Humphrey interjected.

"Nothing at all?"

"No. I had Bradford even call up a fella that used to work with Earl on a part-time basis and he's pretty sure he never had any sort of dealings with either Wendy Pullman or this new guy, Gary Anderson."

"Yeah, but the former employee *knew* of Gary Anderson. Said the little bit he knew about the guy painted him as a Grade-A asshole."

"What about Lizzi Stone?" Palmer asked. "Any connection between her and Pullman or Stewart?"

"If there are, it's so minuscule that it's not going to be found in reports or records," Bradford said.

"So maybe we're looking at this all wrong," Camille said. "We need to think of this as more of a puzzle than a list of victims."

Humphrey and Bradford both nodded as they mulled it over.

"Think of it this way," Camille said. "The killer is the puzzle. And the victims are the pieces. Connecting the victims to the killer will give us the picture."

"So how do we figure out who the bigger picture is?" Humphrey asked. "And what's in it?"

"Well let's think of the sort of people that might feel comfortable being around alligators," Camille said. "People unlike Carl Griffin. Are there people that live in the area that might run into gators, or at least *see* them more than the average person? Someone that might not really even be all that bothered any the sight of them because they're seen so often?"

"No one specific comes to mind," Humphrey said after a while. "But I'd start looking closer to the bayou. Even out there, it's not a given that you'll see gators, but it's much more likely."

"So let' start looking at that. Someone that knows the bayou area well. Well enough to traverse it at night and know where to find alligators without much trouble. Someone that can slip in and out of hiding with relative ease. And someone that knows how to lure people to him."

"If you're truly looking in that direction," Humphrey said, "then I think you can forget about anyone working at reserves or even people like Carl Griffin...someone that trains them. From the looks of the bodies, these are wild gators. Not a speck of domestication to them."

"So where can we start looking?" Camille asked. "Is there an area anywhere around here that fits that description?"

"Well, there's Bayou Saint John," Bradford said. "But I don't think any of those areas would be conducive to the sort of person you're talking about. Those are all pretty population dense areas. It's much more likely you'd see someone like that out in the boonies."

"We're going to need to think of a way to narrow that search down," Camille said. "Narrow it down to manageable chunks."

"I'll start running the records, then," Bradford said. He got to his feet and started for the door.

"Hey, hold on," Humphrey said. "I think we can maybe skip the record-searching. You remember that cantankerous old fart Miles Simpson?"

Bradford had to think about it for a moment, but slowly nodded. "Yeah, I remember him. Drunk and disorderly a few times a few years back. Something about his ex-wife, right?"

"Pull the report, would you?" Humphrey said.

Bradford nodded and hurried out, leaving the other three to sit in the hopeful expectation of this new direction.

"This Bayou Saint John place," Palmer said. "What's it like?"

"Imagine a trailer park, but sort of chopped up and scattered all along the woods," Humphrey said. "That's was we're talking about. A series of small, backwoods shacks all along the swamps. We'll get a few meth busts in the area once or twice a year."

"Any murders or violent assaults in the area within the past year or so?"

"The only actual murder I can recall was a fisherman that caught his wife and her boyfriend with his pants down in the middle of the bayou. But that's been three years ago. Every now and then we'll get a domestic dispute call, and the gas station will get robbed about once every six months. That sort of thing."

Camille was about to ask another question, but Bradford came walking back into the room. He was carrying a laptop and wore an expression of restrained excitement on his face.

"That was quick," Palmer commented.

"Well, with a name to already go on, it was easy to find." Bradford palmed the laptop in the center of the table and nodding toward it. "This is what I found about Simpson. He was arrested for disorderly conduct after a drunken fight with his ex-wife. He threw a trash can through a window at the local store when she refused to speak to him."

"He's just a grumpy old drunk right down at the heart of it," Humphrey said, "but I don't see him killing these guys. But maybe he saw something."

"I was thinking the same thing, but there's a note right here in the file...something he said when he was arrested."

The three of them waited as Bradford grinned nervously. "He says, and I quote: 'I should have just tied the bitch up and fed her to the gators in my back yard.'"

Palmer chuckled and got to his feet. "Yeah, so what's his address? I think it might be worth paying him a visit."

Camille thought so, too. At first, the connection seemed tenuous at best. but then again…it was small community. A man that knew all three victims, had close interactions with gators, and had shown a tendency towards violence in the past was a perfect match. So, with that thought in mind, as far as Camille was concerned, they had their next lead.

***

Humphrey had given a fitting description of the area. The paved road that led to Bayou Saint John came to an abrupt end, the one warning coming in the form of an old, rusty END STATE MAINTENANCE sign. The road then became a dirt track that looked more like something Camille would expect to see in the bush areas of Africa. The road itself was well worn, but the swampy forest hugged it tightly.

As she glanced ahead, she watched as several bugs splattered against the windshield.

"Well, this is charming," Palmer said.

They passed by the first house along the road, a dilapidated shack in the center of a mostly-dead lawn. Three well-used lawn chairs sat in the yard, one tilted over and mostly rusted. A mangey dog lay on the porch, barely raising is head to watch them as they passed by.

Camille had seen communities like this before, a few times in her childhood. She had never been the type to look down on people because of the way they lived and she didn't start now. But she also knew that a location like this was a very attractive draw for people looking to engage in nefarious activities.

Another half a mile, after passing by three more poorly maintained homes, she turned left. From what Humphrey had told them, there would be only two houses down this stretch of road, the last one belonging to their person of interest, Miles Simpson.

The first of the two homes they passed was a rusted-out, old trailer. Camille was sure that anything alive inside had been there for less than one month. She could almost feel the bugs crawling up her legs as they passed by.

After a slight bend in the road, the trail now thinning out a bit, they came to the last house on this stretch. Oddly enough, it was in much better shape than the others they'd passed ever since leaving the paved road behind. It was a modular home, its white vinyl having nearly turned a peculiar shade of yellow. The thick wall of trees behind it looked so green and lush that they almost appeared black. A small barn sat very close to the house; a tattered old pickup truck was parked directly between the two structures.

Camille parked and got out. She could smell swamp in the air, could feel a softening sort of give to the ground under her feet as they made their way to a rectangular concrete block that served as the porch.

It was quiet out here, so quiet she could hear the very slight breeze rustling through the trees and the buzzing of bees that were far enough away that she couldn't even see them.

She raised her hand to knock on the door but paused. She could hear something else as well...a strange sound, almost like something slithering. It was coming from the back of the house...not a slithering, but a scraping.

"You hear that, too?" Palmer whispered.

Camille nodded and stepped back down into the yard. She strayed around the side of the house, hand hovering over her Glock. She came around the corner just in time to see a man slipping out of a window. He'd just dropped down to his feet, nearly stumbling, when Camille came around the back corner.

"Mr. Simpson?"

The man looked over his shoulder, his eyes wide with fear. He looked old, as they'd been told, maybe around seventy or so. He was also skinny and frail; yet, when he took off at a run, Camille found that he was also deceptively fast.

"Mr. Simpson! Stop! FBI!"

He didn't look back. Instead, he ran directly ahead, straight toward the forest. Camille nearly pulled her gun to shoot a warning shot, but figured that might be a bit much.

Palmer hurried around to her side and cursed under his breath. "He's a fast old bastard, huh?"

"Hopefully not too fast," Camille said. And with that, she let out a frustrated sigh and took off after him.

CHAPTER TWENTY TWO

It only took a few seconds for Camille to regret not firing a warning shot. Within a few steps of entering the dense forest, she knew she was going to have a hell of a time on her hands. She could hear the man, presumably Miles Simpson, moving somewhere through the thick growth ahead, but everything was so tightly wound together out here that it was difficult to pinpoint an exact direction.

Vines, leaves, and cobwebs slapped her in the face as she did her best to follow the noise. Palmer fell in behind her, cutting slightly to the right.

"He went this way, right?" he said, nodding ahead of him.

"I thought it was this way," she said, pointing slightly to her left.

"Christ, this is a mess. Was he doing anything, or was he just making a run for it?"

"I just saw him running."

"How about you go that way and I'll go over here?" he said, again nodding back in his direction of choice.

"We'll get lost in this mess, get separated."

"Okay," Palmer said, shaking his head. "Or we could just stand here and argue about it."

"Fine. Split up. Shout out if you catch him or need assistance."

"Yup," he said, and took off in his direction.

Camille headed forward, still listening to the sounds of Simpson rushing through the forest. The ground was boggy, not quite mud but close enough to make running a bit tricky. Simpson, on the other hand, was running like he knew the woods a little too well...like he did this sort of thing all of the time.

"Simpson! Damn it, stop right now!"

The sound of movement further ahead of her, growing a bit farther away now, made it clear that he would do no such thing. However, as Camille scrambled forward, she saw a freshly snapped sapling to her right. Directly ahead of it, the thin branch of another small tree was flapping a bit, as if something large had just passed by it.

She bound ahead, dodging low-hanging branches and sidestepping stumps and logs. She started to hear a wet squishing sound as the ground got even muddier, the true swamp starting to reveal itself.

Camille started to worry that she was in over her head. She was running directly into an unknown patch of woods that, based on what she knew, might be occupied by alligators. And she was chasing a man that knew the area intimately. Still, she kept moving forward, not sure if she believed she was actually going to find him, but also unwilling to quit now that she was so close.

As she ran, she looked at the ground. It was wet enough now that she could easily see the fresh prints ahead of her. They angled slightly to the left, showing where Simpson was headed. Her eyes on those prints, Camille kicked up her speed, having to leap over a fallen log. Vaguely, she was aware of a bug of some kind buzzing by her head, of another one biting her on the forearm.

But then she saw Miles Simpson directly ahead of her. The old man appeared to already be gassed. She drew her Glock, not intending to use it but to simply scare him with it. She took three more huge strides towards him and saw that he'd come to a stop. He was leaning against a massive, gnarled cypress tree and holding his knee.

"Shit," he said.

"Mr. Simpson, why did you run?"

"Who're you?" he asked, gasping for breath.

"I told you back there at your house, when I was yelling for you," she said. She wasn't holding her Glock on him, but it was slightly raised, aimed in his general direction. "I'm Agent Camille Grace, with the FBI. Now...why did you run?"

He said nothing. He looked scared, a bit puzzled. Camille took another step towards him but she didn't get a chance to say anything else.

A scream tore through the thick forest. Palmer's voice, yelling out in surprise and maybe pain. He was close but, again, the forest made it very hard to determine where he was, exactly.

Working quickly and thinking on her feet, Camille plucked her handcuffs from her belt and approached Simpson. Before he even had a chance to object, Camille had pulled his hands behind his back. She slapped one cuff on him, then gave him a nudge over towards a thin elm tree.

"What the hell are you doin'?" Simpson yelled.

"Stay here. Because we had to chase your stubborn ass through the woods, my partner needs my help."

She locked the cuffs in place with the tree between Simpson's arms. Still winded from his little sprint through the woods, he didn't even bother to argue or fight. He still looked incredibly baffled, staring at the handcuffs as if he expected them to bite him at any moment.

Camille turned to the right and dashed in the direction she assumed Palmer to be. She took a moment to caution herself; she knew that she had to be smarter than this, running blindly through these woods, and couldn't allow herself to get so carried away. Even so, she pushed on, the ground now almost completely soft and pliable under her feet. The smell of damp, sodden earth was thick. She could hear Palmer, his voice uttering a stream of soft curses. She could also hear a splashing noise and then one last curse, a hissed "Fuck."

She came through a thicket of what looked to be kudzu and saw Palmer. She also saw what had happened to him.

He'd slipped from a bank that was hidden by the curtain of kudzu vine. It wasn't a sheer drop off, but it was slanted enough to cause him to slip down it; the mud certainly didn't help, either.

He was two feet below her, on his ass in muddy, black water. At first, she thought he was injured. After all, he wasn't moving. He wasn't even turning to look at her as she toed along the edge of the little drop-off. Instead, he was looking straight ahead.

Camille followed his gaze and her blood went cold.

The top half of an alligator was bobbing in the water less than five feet from him. More than that, it seemed to be slowly gliding towards Palmer. It wasn't a big one, but certainly not a baby, either. She guessed it to be about four feet long from snout to tail.

She saw him reaching for his sidearm, a totally logical reaction to the situation...but a reaction that she also knew could be deadly.

Don't do it, she thought. *Don't you dare...*

She thought about something she'd heard many years ago as a girl at Deanna's house. It was the same bit of advice she'd often heard in regards of what to do if you were ever attacked by a shark.

Slowly, she eased herself into the water. The gator's nostrils were flared; it let out a brief grunt as it turned its attention to her.

She inched towards it, raising her right hand slowly and shaping it into the form of a palm-strike. As the gator's eyes took her in, she couldn't believe she was doing this. She felt a bit like she was invincible but also like she may piss her pants.

Too late to crawl out now, she thought.

With a lunge to the right, out of the direct line of the beast's jaws, she shaved her hand forward. Her palm struck the gator directly in the snout. As soon as she connected, she drew back and delivered it again.

The gator whipped itself around in retreat, ducking its head underwater and slapping its tail all around. The moment it reared away, Camille reached down and helped Palmer to his feet. They both hurried back up the bank, crashing through the kudzu.

"Are you kidding me?" Palmer said. "You...Grace, you just punched an alligator."

"No, I struck it on its snout. Big difference." She had to make a joke out of it because her nerves were still rocketing out of control. What in the hell had she been thinking? If she'd slipped the slightest bit in the muck at the bottom of that water, she may be missing a right hand right now.

"I don't even..." Palmer said. He ran a shaking, muddy hand through his hair. "Thanks, Grace. That was...well, that was pretty amazing."

"Let's get out of here, though," she said. "If it comes back, I don't have the nerve to try it again."

"You get Simpson?"

"Yeah, he's a hugging a tree right now."

"He's...what?"

"Just come on."

She led him back the way she'd come, looking back over her shoulder at the murky water for any sign of the gator. And even though it was nowhere to be seen, every muscle in her body wanted to get the hell out of those woods as soon as possible.

CHAPTER TWENTY THREE

The adrenaline that came with punching an alligator had worn off by the time Camille and Palmer made it back to the Hen Creek police station. The sudden absence of adrenaline left Camille with an odd sort of weariness, almost as if she could take a nap.

Bradford took Simpson from them when they came into the station, allowing Camille to retreat to the little coffee station in the far back corner. Bradford gave her a cringing stare, noting that both she and Palmer were soaked, and that their shoes were very muddy.

In the back, Camille ran the darkest brew they had through their instant-cup maker and chugged about half of it down.

"You okay?" Palmer asked her.

"Yeah, just wiped out. And soaked."

"You punched a gator in the face. You're allowed to be wiped out."

"Don't expect that sort of treatment in the future," she said. "Looking back on it, it was a pretty bone-headed move."

"Bone-headed, bad-ass...whichever works for you," Palmer said. "So, are you ready to go speak with our new friend?"

"Might as well," she said, chugging more of the bitter coffee.

They found Bradford waiting for them at the door to the interrogation room. "You guys good?" he asked.

"Sure," Palmer said. "Hey, this one right here," he said, nudging Camille, "punched a gator in the face."

"What?"

Camille shook her head and opened the interrogation room door. Palmer followed her in and after closing the door, they looked down to Miles Simpson. He had the look of a kid that had just been caught looking at a dirty movie.

"Why'd you run?" Camille asked him.

"And why'd you run in the direction of where there were gators?" Palmer asked, irritated. "It almost seems like you did it on purpose."

"I ran because I didn't want to get into trouble."

"And why do you think you would have been in trouble?" Palmer asked.

"Well, you two are clearly detectives, or feds, right?"

"Feds," Camille said. "Agents Grace and Palmer, with the FBI. So again...what have you done lately that might warrant a visit from us?"

She felt almost optimistic. Was it going to be this easy? Was Simpson their guy? Was he seriously about to cop to all of it this easily just because a visit from two federal agents had spooked him?

Simpson eyed them with that same guilt in his eyes and then gave a defeated shrug. "I violated my parole two different times."

"Your parole?" Palmer said. And then, realizing he'd nearly showed their ignorance about his past, he quickly recovered. "And how did you do that, Mr. Simpson?"

"The restraining order on my ex-wife." Scant understanding started to show on his face. "Wait...you weren't there for that?"

"No, Mr. Simpson, we weren't," Camille said. "We came to visit you because of a very specific threat you made when you had that bit of trouble a few years ago with your ex. A comment about gators. You know what we're talking about, right?"

He nodded and looked back down to the table as he recited the line. "I should have just tied the bitch up and fed her to the gators in my backyard."

"That's the one," Palmer said.

"Have there always been alligators that close to your property?" Camille asked.

She watched as Miles Simpson tried to understand why he was sitting in an interrogation room. Now that they'd told him their visit had nothing to do with his wife or an apparent restraining order against her, he seemed very confused. Sure, it could all be an act, but Camille didn't see anything particularly calculated about his behavior.

"Yeah," he finally answered. "And it gets worse when it rains. They come a little further outside of the swamps after a heavy rain."

"And it doesn't bother you to live that close to them?" Camille asked.

"They'll shy away after a while."

"After what?" Palmer asked.

"After they've had their fill of whatever they're after... or if they get bored. Gators aren't very smart. They might try to get up on your deck or your patio, but they always give up after a while."

"But it doesn't bother you?" Camille asked.

"I've lived here my whole life. Gators are part of the landscape. I see one from my porch all the time. I've never had one try to get in."

"Ever had a dangerous run-in with one?"

"A few times. I damn near stepped on one as a teenager. But even then, it didn't attack."

"Mr. Simpson, I'm going to give you three names," Camille said. "I need you to tell me if any of them ring any bells. Can you do that?"

"Sure." He seemed instantly relieved that the interrogation was taking a turn that led further away from his ex-wife.

"Wendy Pullman. Earl Stewart. Gary Anderson."

"I know who Gary Anderson is, but I don't *know* him, if you know what I mean. But that mean old bastard, I guess everyone knows *of* him, at least. And the name Earl Stewart...that sticks out for some reason but I couldn't tell you why." He shrugged and said, "I mean, it's a small county. You're bound to hear just about everyone's name after a while, you know?"

Based on the ease at which he'd answered and the lack of any sort of facial expression at hearing the names, Camille was all but certain Miles Simpson was not their killer. But she also wasn't quite ready to let him go due to his admission of violating a restraining order, as well as the hell she and Palmer had gone through to bring him in.

"And if we asked you, would you be able to provide proof of your whereabouts over the last few nights?"

Simpson thought about this for a moment and shrugged. "I don't know. Depends on what you need. I've literally been sitting around my house, drinking beer and watching TV."

"What have you been watching?" Palmer asked.

"There's a show on National Geographic where they drop Gordon Ramsey off in these random places and he cooks with local ingredients." He seemed perplexed that they'd ask him this, chuckling as he came to a stop.

Camille knew that a quick trip through his Recently Watched would be able to back up the story. And even if that failed, they could send in a request to find out where his phone had been resting for the last few nights. But really, she didn't think it would come to that.

"Mr. Simpson, thank you for your time," she said. "We're going to have Officer Bradford come in and ask you some questions about your whereabouts over the last few days."

He still seemed a little confused, but he nodded all the same. Camille exited the room, wondering how they'd so quickly come to yet another dead end. Idly, she figured that they'd eventually run out of people that had some sort of connection to alligators. And then what?

Palmer joined her out in the hallway. He also looked a little tired and run down. The filthy clothes certainly didn't help.

"Well, he's no killer, that's for sure," Palmer said.

"Yeah, I'd say it's doubtful."

"I do think we may be on to something with looking in that area, though," Palmer said. "There was a whole lot of nothing, sure, but it would be the perfect place to stash bodies. It's like a whole other world out there. However, I don't know about you, but I intend to change out of these clothes first. Did you pack a change?"

"I did. And that's actually a good idea. Maybe if I can get out of these mucky clothes and grab a shower, it'll be easier to find a new approach."

"And I'd like to have this thing solved and be back on our way home for good before Captain Beecher decides he wants to suddenly be involved again."

"And at this rate," Camille said, "there's just no telling when another body is going to pop up."

"Yeah, that, too."

Camille left the hallway to find Bradford, her feet squishing in her wet shoes the whole way. Frowning, she thought the feeling and the sound of it was a pretty good summation of this entire case up to this point.

***

Grabbing a shower back at Newcomb's Motel did indeed help her a bit more than she'd expected. Before getting in, Camille kicked off her shoes, dried them out as well as she could, and left them out on the little walkway outside of the rooms to dry off in the thick Louisiana heat.

When she was out and dried off, she got dressed and realized that showering so early on such a humid day may be counter-productive. But at least she had the feel of the swamp from behind Miles Simpson's house off of her.

She stepped out onto the walkway to check her shoes. They were still damp, but a vast improvement from before she'd kicked them off. They'd surely start stinking in a few days but hopefully she'd be back in New Orleans by then.

Before sticking her feet back into them, she found herself thinking of her father. Seeing him had still not quite registered with her; it had almost been like watching a movie and recalling certain scenes. But at the same time, she thought it might be a movie worth watching again.

She headed back inside and grabbed up her phone, intending to call him. But as the phone was in her head, it was Deanna she suddenly found herself thinking of. Deanna had kept two alligator statues on one of her many bookshelves...not ceramic statues, but wood carvings. Camille could remember, even from her childhood, that the etchings and carvings along the back to represent the scaly skin had always sort of unnerved her as a young girl. Deanna had said she kept the wood carvings because, while she thought gators were cool and sort of mystic in a way, she was always terrified of them.

Curious, Camille pulled up Deanna's number and called her. The woman had always been a well of information on the most random things. Maybe she knew a thing or two about gators, too. And maybe getting insights from someone three hours way from the current crime scene would offer a fresh perspective.

Deanna answered on the second ring. She sounded slightly out of breath when she said, "Hello?"

"Hey, D. It’s Camille."

"Oh, hey! How are you?"

"I'm good."

"I was starting to wonder, seeing as how you haven't bothered to call a single time after your initial call to tell me you were back in Louisiana."

"Sorry about that. I've been setting up the new office and all, and then got put on this case."

"Anything fun?"

"Fun isn't quite the word I would use. But some of the details did bring to mind those two old gators you used to have on your bookshelves. The wooden ones."

"Oh, I still have them. And....you're on a case concerning gators?"

"Yeah, it's a long story. But I just need...I don't know. I need a different angle on this whole thing. I remember you were really scared of them but also thought they were beautiful."

"Yeah, and that still very much remains the same."

"Can you walk me through that? How can you feel two ways about them? And is there anything you know about Louisiana gators that might not be in textbooks or nature reserves?"

She could hear Deanna smile on the other line. "Okay. Well, gators were very big in Louisiana culture, especially in the Deep South. They were seen as a symbol of power and strength not too long ago, you know. I don't know all the history, but from what I heard from grandparents and aunts and uncles, the Native Americans respected gators as the protectors of their homes and the land. There's this whole spiritual connection to it. The swamp and the swamp's reputation for hiding everything, including people, also played a part in it. But seeing as how they are a symbol of strength, it was thought that seeing one showed you had a very strong, watchful guardian."

"What about maybe as a means of vengeance?" Camille asked.

"I don't think I've ever heard of anything like that. Jesus, what kind of a case is this?"

"I'll tell you some other time. It's currently open and there are three bodies. it's pretty bad."

"Three bodies? God, what's going on? And where are you, anyway?"

"Hen Creek."

"Oh. Oh, wow. Yeah, that's way out in the sticks. Makes Upping look like New York City."

"That's pretty accurate."

"Is this some kind of hazing thing?" Deanna asked. "Did your new bosses send you down there to deal with gators as some sort of punishment?"

"No, it just happened to—"

Camille stopped here, replaying Deanna's previous comment. *Some sort of punishment...*

"Yeah?" Deanna said. "Just happened to what?"

"D, I have to go. But you have my word...I'll call you back as soon as the case is over."

"You'd better. And you need to get over to see your Dad."

"Already ahead of you on that. And we can talk more about that when I call, too. Thanks, Deanna."

"Same to you. Be careful out there...you know...around all those gators." She said it with a sarcastic edge, as if she thought Camille might be pulling her leg a bit in terms of what the case was centered around.

"Some sort of punishment," Camille said. She thought of Deanna being scared of gators but respecting them in her own way by keeping her woodcarvings on the bookshelf. What if someone else felt the same way about them? What if their killer feared them and, as such, felt that a fitting punishment for someone they thought deserved judgement of some kind was to feed them to gators?

It was messed up on multiple levels but, given the nature of this case, also made a small bit of sense. If their killer had once been attacked by a gator at some point in their life and was experiencing hardship or troubles from it, wouldn't it only make sense that they would view gators as a means of retribution or even judgement?

A knock on the door broke her concentration, but that was fine; the gist of a possible new approach was already there. She answered the door and found Palmer standing on the walkway. His hair was still slightly wet, and she saw that he'd also shaved away the tiny growth of stubble that had accumulated on his face. Standing in the sun and giving her a casual smile, he looked quite handsome.

"You good to go?" he asked.

"I am. And I think I figured out a new approach we can take. Maybe a way to narrow down the search for our suspect."

"That's great."

She stepped outside, locking the door behind her. She slipped her feet into the still-damp shoes.

"Back to the station?" Palmer asked.

"For now, yes, I think so."

"Okay. Oh, and Grace?"

"Yeah?"

"Do something about those shoes, will you?" he said, the smile on his face growing wider. "They're really starting to reek."

CHAPTER TWENTY FOUR

He knew it was too early to start drinking. it wasn't even 3:00 in the afternoon yet. And he had some work to do later in the night.

But Christ, it was hot. Some days it just got so humid that you *had* to drink. he knew the Budweisers he'd been pounding lately did nothing to hydrate him, but he *felt* as if they did. Also, drinking steeled up his nerves.

It had also helped him to forget about how he looked, over the years. He'd started drinking heavily at the age of sixteen. It had helped him to not care about how bad he was teased, how bad he looked, and how much his father and brother had teased him.

Everyone had teased him, though. It was screwed up because if he'd had some sort of disability from birth, he didn't think he would have been treated as such. But no...he'd always been the idiot kid that had gone out into the woods and stumbled across a gator.

Things would have probably been better if he'd just been killed that day. Sometimes he wished it *had* happened that way.

But now that he'd come to terms with his life, he figured the one thing he could do was to take control. The people that had made his life so miserable were now being punished in a way fitting of their crimes.

Back in his little hideaway by the swamp, he sat on the tailgate of his truck, drinking a beer and thinking over the last week or so.

There was no real order to it. He'd simply gone after them in the order he thought would be easiest.

Earl Stewart had been first. The mean old bastard that had fired him because the kids of one of his clients had been scared of the way he looked, the side of his face all knotted and twisted.

Then there was Wendy Pullman—the woman that had agreed to meet him for a date and then sputtered some bullshit excuse about needing to leave the moment she saw the right side of his face.

Gary Anderson had been an easy choice, too. Gary had been a senior in high school when he'd been a freshman. The bastard had relentlessly tormented him, going so far as to shove his head in a toilet already filled with excrement, yelling to him that there were gators in this particular swamp and they wanted the rest of their meal. Gary had continued his antics until well after high school, the most recent assault coming just eight months ago when Gary had laughed at him when they'd passed one another in the convenience store. As if that waste of space was better than him.

And the next...well, the next one was his own kin. Taking care of this particular problem was going to be tricky. He wasn't sure if he'd be able to pull it off, actually.

Another swig of beer reassured him that he could do it. It would be messy and there would probably be some crying, but he could do it.

And it would be done tonight.

He knew where to strike. He'd reached out just to make sure, sent a text and asked if he could tag along. It would be out at his favorite fishing spot—the very same spot his father had taken him to when he was only seven years old and he'd seen his first gator up close, the same spot his father had taken him after his mother had died. A spot just a mile or so away from where he'd nearly been killed by the gator that had made his life a living hell.

One more night, one more feeding. One more death.

And then he'd get out of this miserable place. Looking back, it was something he should have done as soon as he was able. He could have left this county, this entire state, and gone somewhere else.

Maybe even back then, before he'd even thought of running away, he'd known he was meant to stay. Had he been planning this revenge out for this long? Had he buried this last murder in more recent victims like Earl, Wendy, and Gary because he *knew* this last one would close this wretched chapter?

Maybe so. Actually, he hoped so. That, at least, would make the murders almost poetic. And if this was something his life that had been leading towards completion since that gator sunk its teeth into him all those years ago, then he thought he could live the rest of his life in peace, even after all of the killing.

CHAPTER TWENTY FIVE

Camille stood in front of the small conference room and regarded Palmer and Humphrey, the only other two people in the room. Bradford and Swanson were out on patrol, Bradford having just released Miles Simpson with a warning about his parole. It really didn't matter, though; for what she had in mind, it shouldn't take too long—if this was the right path to take at all.

"Let's forget about people that might have past records," she said. "And let's forget about people that might have easy access to gators. I want to know how we can find a list of people that have been *attacked* by gators."

"Forgive me," Humphrey said, "but how is that going to help?"

"If our killer has been attacked by a gator in the past, he's going to have a healthy fear of them, but a degree of respect, too. And if he's been attacked in the past, he'd see them as a form of punishment. Maybe he's giving these victims over to the gators because he feels they need to be punished."

"That would make sense," Palmer said. "We've already said that depending on the killer's viewpoint, all three of our victims could have been seen as a bully. Even Wendy Pullman, whose bullying would have been passive or not even real bullying at all but just *seen* as bullying."

"But we checked the dating profiles," Humphrey said. "Nothing on that app pointed to anything helpful."

"Well, if someone has been attacked by a gator bad enough and is bearing the scars of it, do you think they'd even use a dating app? Think about the profile picture situation alone."

"Could have been…*gasp*…an old-fashioned, traditional date," Palmer said.

"Okay, then," Humphrey said. "A hospital isn't going to do any good. No way they're going to release medical records so easily. And even if they do, it'll be a few days. I think for this sort of information, our best bet is the Louisiana Department of Wildlife and Fisheries. They get reports of all animal attacks: gators, foxes, bears, snakes, raccoons..."

"Raccoons?" Palmer asked, snickering.

"You laugh, but a rabid raccoon will jack you up pretty good," Humphrey said.

"So that's where we'll start," Camille said. "Humphrey do you have any connections over at the Department of Wildlife and Fisheries that can help us expedite things?"

Humphrey smiled and winked at her. "I happen to be on good terms with the secretary there. I'll give him a call."

He headed out, leaving Camille and Palmer in the conference room alone.

"You ever work a case this strange?" Camille asked.

"You mean, aside from the voodoo-related one you and I tackled a few weeks ago?"

"Yeah, besides that."

He smirked and seemed to look inward, really diving into his memories. "Yeah, there was one. A spooky damn case, in fact. Five bodies were found at a campground out near Baton Rouge about three years ago. Each body's face had been partially skinned and someone had tried screwing deer antlers onto their heads. When we finally found the guy, turns out he was a taxidermist that had lost his entire family in a car crash four months earlier. But the hunt for the guy took a while. And every site where we were sure we were going to nab him, we'd find a half-gutted deer carcass."

"That's...horrible."

"Yeah, it was." When he shrugged, Camille could see him shake the memory of it away. "What about you?"

"Nothing like that. Nothing weird or strange, only...there was this one time in Birmingham where a seven-year-old had been so badly neglected by her parents that by the time we found her, she was pretty much dead. I was there in the hospital when she slipped away and she kept talking about the 'shiny people in the corner.' I never saw them but...I got chills. And I had them for about five minutes after she died."

Palmer shook his head and gave a nervous smile. He then showed Camille his arms, where goosebumps had broken out.

"Hey, what do you think about this whole thing between us?" he asked.

"What do you mean? You mean working as partners?"

"No, I meant the obvious sexual tension." He chuckled and said, "Yes, I meant working as partners."

"I could see it. I'm not going to make such a request so early working under McCutcheon, though."

Palmer was about to respond when Humphrey came back into the room. He had his cellphone to his head and as he sat down at the desk, he said: "Okay, so listen, Harvey. I've got the agents right here."

He took the phone away from his face and placed it on speaker mode.

"Okay, Harvey, you're on."

"Hey, agents. Harvey Pilgrim here, over at Wildlife and Fisheries. I was just telling Humphrey that your hunt for gator attacks is a really easy one. How far you need me to go back?"

"Not sure," Camille said. "Maybe twenty years?"

"I'm on the database right now and I already went back twenty-five. I'm looking at just four reported gator attacks in your county and fifteen in the entire state."

"Okay, let's just start with the county," Camille said.

"Well, of the four, only three are viable because one of these folks was killed from the attack. Now, I understand you're working with Humphrey there down in Hen Creek...and one of these attacks comes from right there, in that town, fourteen years ago."

Of course it does, she thought. Feeling an excited tension growing as the case seemed to slowly come together right before her, she asked: "Any details on it?"

"Just about how the attack happened. I don't have much on the actual victim. The name was Harlan, a fifteen-year-old male. He was helping his father trap gators. It was later learned that they were doing it to sell to a third party that was buying gators for hides and meat."

"What was the extent of the attack?"

"A bite along the back of the calf that required stitches. A big gouge along the base of the right shoulder, too. The father got nicked, too, but he didn't file a report. I don't even see here where there are any hospital reports for him. Must have been pretty minor."

"Got a name on the father?"

But before Harvey Pilgrim could answer, Humphrey did. "If the last name is Harlan, the father is going to be Reed Harlan. Father of Anthony and Kyle. Anthony is something of a local shit-kicker, sort of in the style of Gary Anderson."

"And he lives in Hen Creek?" Palmer asked.

"Just outside of Hen Creek, yeah."

"You know the way?" Camille asked.

Humphrey grinned and picked up his phone. "Thanks, Harvey," he said. "We'll take it from here."

***

It was a short drive yet, somehow, the stretch of forest they had to enter felt like a different world altogether. There was no one at home at Kyle Harlan's residence and since Humphrey had no idea where Anthony Harlan lived, they tried Reed, the father.

Reed Harlan lived in a cabin that looked to be on its last legs but also had a sort of rustic charm to it. It reminded Camille far too much of the house she'd visited her father in. The house was down a thin, dirt driveway. All along the sides of the driveway there was scattered debris that seemed to have no real rhyme or reason to it, some of it mostly hidden by towering weeds: a stack of old tires, a small dog pen, a junked pickup truck that was at least thirty years old, a pile of old plywood pallets.

The house sat at the back of it all on a lawn that was surprisingly well-maintained. A structure that was either a small barn or a large shed sat off to the right of the property. The double doors were open, and a small Nissan pickup sat half-parked inside. A mangey looking dog sat on the porch, perking its head up as Camille brought their sedan to a stop at the end of the driveway, next to a very old car.

As Camille and Palmer stepped out, a man came walking out of the shed to their right. He stopped at the back of the Nissan and watched then, not saying a word. He was wearing a pair of dirty jeans and a backwards baseball cap. He wore no shirt, revealing a tattoo of a tribal design on his right arm and a considerable amount of scarring on his left shoulder. Given that he couldn't be any older than thirty-five—forty at most—Camille assumed this was Anthony Harlan.

Anthony was holding a hammer in his right hand and a beer bottle in his left.

"You folks lost?" Anthony finally said.

"I don't think so," Palmer said. He seemed to take quick strides to assume the lead, mainly because of Anthony's gruff look. Camille appreciated it and allowed him to take it. "Are you Anthony Harlan?"

"Depends on who's asking."

"Does your name change based on who's asking for it?" Palmer asked. He then took out his ID and showed it to Anthony as they approached the shed. "We're agents Palmer and Grace, FBI. We were actually hoping to speak with your father. This is his place, right?"

"Maybe."

Camille took a quick look around, just making sure Reed Harlan *wasn't* here and trying to escape somewhere. The last thing she wanted was to take another run through these unpredictable woods.

"Well, based on information the Hen Creek PD has given us, we believe it is," Camille said. "And there's no need to be difficult. We legitimately just want to ask him some questions."

"About what?"

Camille nearly took over but gave Palmer a few seconds to push the conversation along. "We're investigating a string of murders that are being staged to look like alligator attacks. We understand that both you and your father have both suffered attacks. From the same gator, right?"

"That's right," Anthony said bitterly. He then turned his left shoulder to them, as if in defiance. The scarring was very evident but had healed nicely. "Did a hell of a job, didn't it?" he then turned his eyes to Camille and grinned. "I'd have to take my pants off to show you the other mark. Need me to do that for you?"

"Hey, Anthony," Palmer said. "None of that. And that's your only warning. We clear?"

Anthony smirked and sipped from his bottle of beer.

"Is your father here?"

"Nope."

"Any idea where he is?"

"Somewhere."

Camille was about to lose her patience. She could see that Palmer was struggling, too.

"Mr. Harlan," Camille said, "there's no need to be difficult. You're going to make what could be an easy situation into a really bad one if you keep it up. So just let us ask some questions, okay?"

"About the gator attack from twelve years ago...or however frigging long it's been? What the hell for?"

"If you want some real talk," Palmer said, "it's so we can rule him out as a suspect."

"The hell you talking about?" Anthony said. Camille saw the hammer twitch in his hands. "Suspect? For what? These murders you're talking about?"

"It's a convoluted case," Camille said. "We're taking the time to speak with anyone that has experience in gator attacks in the area. Our visit today doesn't mean we think he did it. So where can we find him?"

"Nah, I'm not helping. My dad doesn't need to be caught up in this shit."

"Fine, then will *you* answer some questions?" Palmer asked.

"Not likely."

"How about this, then?" Camille asked. "You either answer some very basic questions right here, right now, or you can answer them from behind the table inside of an interrogation room at the Hen Creek PD."

"You threatening me?" Anthony said. "Because I'm telling you—"

"I'm not threatening you, Mr. Harlan," Camille said. "It's no threat at all if I do things by the book. We need to speak to your father. And if you won't tell us where we can find him, we need you to answer questions. And your refusal to help in either regard means you're essentially obstructing this case. And with three bodies already, the local and state PD aren't going to like that."

"And you think I care." Anthony then took a few steps toward Palmer. His voice was deep and rough as he started his diatribe. "I know my rights. You have no probable cause. You have no warrant."

He was just a few steps away from Palmer now, and he was still clutching the hammer.

"Mr. Harlan," Camille said, "I suggest you either back up or drop that hammer."

Anthony looked to both of them and shook his head, still smirking. He then finished off the bottle of beer and when he was done, he tossed the empty bottle directly at Palmer's feet.

"Or what?" he said. "This is my father's property and I'll be damned if you're going to bully me around on it. So maybe you just leave."

"Seriously," Palmer said. "Why are you being this difficult? You can't be this stupid, right? You're only going to—"

"What'd you call me?" Anthony interrupted.

He raised the hammer and though Camille really didn't think he'd have the balls to use it, she wasn't going to take chances.

She placed her hand on her Glock and shook her head. "No, Mr. Harlan. Drop the hammer."

"Fuck you both," Anthony said.

And then he spit in Palmer's face.

By the book or not, that was too much. Camille took two quick steps forward, her hand still on the Glock.

"Oh, you gonna shoot me? Really? Over that?"

Before she could answer, Palmer took advantage of the distraction. He threw a hard punch to Anthony's gut. The man went over at once, hunched as if he were going to puke. And as soon as Palmer lunged in again, Anthony slung the hammer around in a wide arc. Palmer blocked it easily and when he did, Camille came in and grabbed Anthony's right wrist. She wrenched it hard and she could feel the bones groaning. Anthony yelled out in pain as he dropped the hammer to the ground.

"I'll sue your asses!" Anthony said. "You can't—"

Palmer stepped forward, shoving Anthony hard. He stumbled back to the truck and when he rebounded off of it, he threw a wide haymaker.

Palmer dodged it, caught the assailing arm, and twisted it. Anthony was forced to turn and when he did, Camille was there with the assist. She threw a forearm into the space between Anthony Harlan's bare shoulder blades, pushing him into the back of the truck again. When he still tried to fight them, she planted her knee into the back of Anthony's leg. When his legs buckled, Palmer instinctively used his foot to shove Anthony's feet apart.

He then slapped the handcuffs on Anthony and gave him one final shove. It wasn't until then that he used the sleeve of his shirt to wipe the spit off of his face.

"Congratulations, Mr. Harlan," Palmer said. "You're under arrest."

CHAPTER TWENTY SIX

When they arrived back at the station with Anthony Harlan in custody, Camille thought they may have to call for an assist to get him inside. She was sure Humphrey or Bradford would be eager to help with such a task. But all it took was a well-delivered elbow to his upper back, dealt out by Palmer, to take most of the fight out of him.

Still, by the time they were in the station and started down the small hallway for the interrogation room, he'd started to buck and go rigid on them. Humphrey was quick to take note and, in the end, he did have to help them usher Anthony into the interrogation room.

"I'll sue everyone in this department!" Anthony said. "This is harassment, plain and simple!"

Camille ignored him but he was continuing to get under Palmer's skin.

"You can't," Palmer said. "If you want to talk to someone about a complaint, you need to contact the FBI. We're just being housed here in Hen Creek. But before you call in with that complaint, you might want to come up with a fitting excuse as to why you spit in a federal agent's face and tried attacking him with a hammer."

This shut Anthony up for a second, his face wrench up in a mask of pure anger.

"You said you were investigating murders," he spat. "And I'm no murderer. And neither is my father."

"Ah, so now he wants to talk," Palmer said.

Camille placed a reassuring hand on Palmer and gave him the gentlest of nudges toward the back wall of the room. He took the hint and stepped away from the table where Anthony Harlan currently sat. Camille stayed where she was, though, looking down at Anthony. He was still without a shirt, the scars from his childhood alligator attack visible. She thought they looked almost like the strange markings some tribal folks placed on themselves—not tattoos, per se, but raised scar-like shapes. She wondered if the gator scars were almost the same sort of branding for Anthony. He'd so quickly made sure to show them off when they'd first visited him. Was he proud of them? Were his scars a badge of honor?

She considered this as she did her best to get him to speak a bit more.

"I understand no one likes to think of their loved ones as murderers," Camille said. "Given that, I get why you might have gotten heated when we insinuated that we wanted to speak to your father about these murders. However, you have to see it through our eyes. You got very defensive. And most people only get that defensive when they're hiding something. So what is it, Anthony?"

"What is what?" he sneered.

"What are you hiding?"

"Nothing! I'm hiding nothing."

"You deny having anything to do with the murders? Or even knowing about them?"

"I didn't know anything about them until you mentioned them. Hell, if anything, I'm the victim here."

Palmer rolled his eyes—Camille could see him from her peripheral vision—but let her lead the interrogation.

Again thinking about how he seemed to be almost proud of his scars, Camille tried a different approach.

"Tell me about your scars. How did that happen?"

"How do you think? It was a gator."

"Well yes, I know that. I'm just curious how a father and son were both attacked at the same time."

"What's that have to do with a murder case?"

"Probably nothing. I'm just trying to get a better feel for how gators behave around here," she said, telling a half-lie. "And what better resource than someone that has been attacked and lived to tell the tale?"

Anthony eyed them skeptically, as if making sure he wasn't being led on. "My dad used to trap them. Capture them, you know? And it's all on public record. He paid fines, did some time, whatever. He used to sell them to this guy down in the bayou."

"And he took you with him when he went out hunting, or trapping?"

"He'd just started. Said I was old enough and that I needed to start earning my keep. So yeah. But I'd been out with him a few times before this happened."

"What do you remember about it?" Camille thought that if she placed the right questions in the right order, she might get him to trip up and admit something; or, on the other hand, he could also manage to give just enough to clear him. Truth be told, she wasn't sure if he was as innocent as he claimed.

When he started talking, she could tell it was a moment he thought about a lot. It was also evident that it was a story he told frequently, likely around bars and poker tables.

"It happened quick. Dad and I had gone out on a boat. We'd gone out the Folsom way, following the canal. We'd gotten pretty deep into the swamp. It was muddy out, I remember. So muddy that Dad almost turned us around and took us somewhere else. We couldn't see more than a few feet in front of us. Then all of a sudden, pop. That was all it was. One second we were going along fine and the next, *pop*. It just slammed right into us."

"And it attacked you right away?"

"Yeah. There was this churning in the water and the next thing I knew, I felt something hard pushing against me while I was I the water. Something hit my dad in the face, and he was just yelping. I thought it was a log or something. Or a log that had just been grabbed by the gator we were following. Then the gator grabs me and pulls me into the water. Took a chunk out of my calf. I tore my leg free and it went for my shoulder. But by that time, my dad had taken his pocket knife out. He jammed the blade right between the gator's eyes. It got him, too, before it retreated out into the water."

As Camille thought of the next question to ask, there was a knock at the door. Palmer opened the door and they saw Humphrey standing there.

"A quick word?" Humphrey said.

The agents exited the room leaving Anthony to revel in his story. In the hallway, Humphrey handed Camille a folder. Inside, there were a few pages of different police reports.

"This is what we have on Anthony Harlan. Like I said, he's a bit of a troublemaker. As you can see, he's got a few drunk and disorderlies, an aggravated assault against a man outside of a bar two months ago. But what really nails it down is this one."

He plucked a sheet out of the thin stack and brought it to the top. Camille read over it and saw a report that had been filed away a year and a half ago. It told of an altercation Anthony had with Gary Anderson in the parking lot of the Hornet's Nest. But another little note near the bottom had a list of four names that had seen the fight and were questioned by the police. One of the names was Wendy Pullman.

"Holy shit," Palmer said. "I'd say that's pretty strong evidence. Great work, Humphrey."

"It seems like strong evidence," Camille said, "but it's a small community. Is it really some astronomical chance that two of our victims and our suspect would just happen to be in the same bar—the *only bar* in the area—at the same time?"

"I think it's more than enough to officially label Anthony Harlan as a suspect for sure," Palmer said. "Especially given his history with gators."

Camille nodded, trying to understand why she wasn't as confident as Palmer and Humphrey. There was something about Anthony's demeanor that was setting queerly with her. It had something to do with his scars and how he was so proud of them. Any sort of pride in disfigurement from the gator attack didn't seem to align with the motives of their killer...whatever those motives may be. If their killer was taking some sort of odd vengeance out on their victims, pride would be the farthest thing from his mind.

"I know it's immature," Palmer said, "but I'd really like to be the one to nail him with this."

"Be my guest," Camille said.

“And you?” he asked.

She took a moment to answer. Something still didn't feel quite right. And if she didn't find out what it was very soon, it might be too late. “I’ll catch up,” she said. “There’s something I want to check on.”

CHAPTER TWENTY SEVEN

Camille sat in the tiny conference room, looking at the dry erase board that Palmer, Humphrey, and Swanson had been using earlier. Many of their old notes remained there, most of them written in Palmer's handwriting. Her eyes remained locked on the names of the victims as she did her best to profile them.

First, there was Earl Stewart. He'd seemed to be a pleasant enough man, respected by most in the community. His only sin was that he was a bit hardnosed when it came to his business. They'd only heard a few cases of this, but it stood to reason that he'd angered at least a few folks he'd worked with.

Wendy Pullman was the hardest to peg down. It was not a crime at all to decline dates with men, or to reject their advances. This was equally true (if not *more true*) when it came to dating apps. But Camille knew that some men took rejection personally, especially if the rejection came as the result of a flaw the men themselves were aware of.

Gary Anderson was, of course, the easiest to profile. In a town this size, anyone that had a bad reputation among the police was sure to have pissed someone off at some point.

When looking at all three of the victims in this light, Camille started to understand that all of the transgressions of the victims were likely not the sort of things they would see as overly hostile in their own eyes. But to a killer, even the slightest grievance could set them off.

She could hear the muffled voices of Anthony Harlan and one of the other officers through the wall as Anthony remained in the interrogation room.

Yes, he'd spit in Palmer's face. And yes, he'd approached them in a threatening manner with a hammer in his hand. And while his police record indicated a tendency towards violence, she knew that didn't make him a killer.

In fact, in this case, she wondered if it made him *less* of a suspect.

If their killer was attacking because of perceived grievances, why involve alligators at all? It was as if the killer was making the gators do the work for him, in the long run.

She felt several of these threads tightening, almost forming a knot that would tie it all in place. She stared at the board, willing it to come out.

"Hey, Grace?"

She turned towards the doorway at the sound of her name. Palmer was standing there with two cups in his hand. He handed one to her and the aroma of coffee filled her head. She really didn't want it, but sipped from it anyway to show her appreciation at the thought.

"So, Anthony is still insisting he did nothing," Palmer said. "He's working his way through the last few nights, giving the cops his alibis."

"And he still won't tell us where his father is?"

"No." Palmer came into the room and sat down at the table with her. "Something wrong?" he asked.

She said it bluntly, as clearly as she could. "I just don't think it's him, Palmer."

He nodded, letting out a small sigh. "Why not?"

She took another sip of coffee, giving herself a moment to further sort out her thoughts. "If the killer was just out killing people, if it was some random serial killer, I'd say Anthony might be a possibility. But the gators don't fit."

"I think the scars on his shoulder say they *do* fit."

"That's just it. Those scars are like a trophy to him. A badge of honor. So for him to use the same creatures that disfigured him in such a way just doesn't line up. Also, think about his record. He doesn't seem the type to go to great lengths. If he wanted to kill someone, I imagined he'd do it. Just swing his hammer, for instance. The extra step of including gators doesn't make sense."

"Do you have anything else to go on? Because they just let Chief Beecher know that we have a suspect in custody. If we change that tune all of a sudden..."

"I don't think we need to change it. But you know...him going out with his father to trap those gators seemed a little strange. Like his father was carelessly endangering a kid, you know?"

"Yeah?"

"It makes me think...when Humphrey and his friend at Fisheries and Wildlife got into the Harlan family, they said Reed Harlan had *two* sons, right?"

"Yeah," Palmer said. "And Anthony was the oldest."

"So imagine you're a kid, growing up with a brother like Anthony. A brother that was almost killed by a gator. Hell, your father, too. Gators, in some way or another, were always a part of this kid's life."

"That's true," Palmer said, a stirring of excitement in his voice.

"Maybe this killer isn't a tormentor," Camille said as the idea truly started to take shape. "Maybe he's been *tormented.* And he's using the gators as a punishment tool."

"It would be all kinds of messed up, but that seems to fit the tone of this case so far."

Camille got to her feet and headed back to the interrogation room. She knocked and didn't wait for an answer. When she walked inside, she saw Bradford taking notes in relation to Anthony Harlan's alibis.

"Can we have the room for a second?" Camille asked.

"Sure thing," Bradford said. He took his notes and left the room. When he was gone, Anthony looked to both of the agents with a bit of fear in his eyes.

"What?" he said.

"What can you tell us about your brother?" Camille asked.

Anthony chuckled and a lopsided grin came to his face. "Kyle? What about him?"

"For starters, did he ever go out on any of these trapping trips with your father?"

"No. After what happened with me and dad, he never let Kyle go out there."

"Do you remember how your brother reacted when you and your father were attacked?"

He laughed and shook his head. "Sure I do. He was mortified. Wouldn't sleep in his own bed for like a year. He was always afraid there was an alligator in his closet or under the bed. Oh, but even though he never went out on one of those trips, the gators still ended up getting to him."

"How so?" Camille asked.

"What do you mean?" Palmer added.

"Huh? What? I figured you already knew, coming in here asking me about that dipshit. Not even two years after me and dad got attacked, he wandered off into the woods and a gator got him. He survived, but he did get messed up. Lost a finger, got some scars. Dad pretty much quit trapping after that. He thought we were cursed or something."

Camille quickly started putting a profile together in her head, going back to what she'd said in the conference room: what if their killer wasn't a tormentor, but had been tormented? Being terrified of gators and then being mauled by one after his father and brother had been?

"Do you happen to know if your brother ever had any dealings with Gary Anderson?"

Again, that stupid laugh of his. "I don't' know about *dealings,"* Anthony said. "But Gary sure did whoop his ass a lot in high school."

Camille felt the pieces starting to click together-the case finally taking a solid shape. She felt the promise of it growing inside of her but wanted to make absolutely certain before she got too excited.

"How about Wendy Pullman?" Palmer ventured.

"Hell if I know. I mean, I think he knew her. She was like a single year ahead of him in school. What does this even have to—"

"Earl Stewart?"

The influx of names seemed to confuse him a bit. Still, he nodded and said, "Well, yeah. Kyle worked for Earl for a while. That was about a year or so ago I guess."

"Was he fired, or did he quit?"

"No clue. But knowing Earl, he probably fired him. I'm not sure how well you know Earl, but he doesn't have much patience. And Kyle is a prime-time screw up."

It was more than enough to redirect Camille's attention to the brother—to Kyle Harlan. Pretty much everything lined up with the profile she'd put together in her mind.

"Where does he live?" Camille asked.

"You're wasting your time. Kyle cries over every damn thing. He's scared of little garden snakes and spiders. No way in hell is he going to—"

"Where?"

"Hell if I know. He was homeless for a while, I think. I just assumed he was always out in that old houseboat Mom used to have."

"What houseboat?" Palmer asked.

"It's been docked up out on this little sliver of swamp mom always used to take Kyle to. Catching fireflies and shit like that."

"How do we get there?"

Enjoying the fact that they were relying on him so heavily, Anthony leaned back in his seat and smiled. "Might want to get some paper and a pen. There's a whole lot of turns and backroads. And GPS won't do a thing for you out where you're headed."

The way he said it sent a chill through her but behind her, Palmer was already heading out of the door in search of a pad and a pen.

CHAPTER TWENTY EIGHT

After hearing where the agents were headed, Camille was relieved when Humphrey offered one of the station's four-wheel drive trucks to venture out into the swampy area. Palmer took the wheel, as he was more experienced with a manual transmission, and it took less than half a mile of off-road country routes for Camille to understand that Anthony Harlan had not been exaggerating.

The first of the several roads on their direction sheet was off of an unmarked stretch of blacktop. The dirt road was thin and apparently one-way only. If they were to meet someone, one of them would have to pull off to the side—and there wasn't much room to allow for such a courtesy.

They were truly out in the middle of nowhere. The roads were firm and well packed with dirt but she knew that the swampier regions were out there, just within walking distance.

Or perhaps they were closer. When Palmer took the first of five turns, the road led down a slight hill and Camille could see standing water not too far away from the edge of the road.

"Question," Palmer said. "Was it just me, or did Anthony seem all too eager to send us off looking for his brother?"

"No, I sensed it, too. Not a peep about where his father is, but was willing to throw his younger brother under the bus."

"I wonder why," Palmer said.

The question hung in the air as he came to another turn. Right away, it was clear that this road was in rougher shape than the others as the swampier regions became more evident.

Palmer slowed the truck and turned at an angle, trying to avoid becoming mired in the soft red dirt of the road. He eased the truck down the road, taking his time as the land was on a slight downward angle. When they reached the bottom of the hill, Camille could see the trees starting to thin out. Through them, she started to see fragments of a body of water. It actually looked rather inviting as the soft golds of the approaching dusk started to fall over the forest and gave a warm hue to everything. Had they not been actively looking for a killer, it may have been a pleasant moment.

The final turns came in quick succession, and the third was essentially nothing more than twin tire-ruts that had been churned into the ground. The water and muck of the swamp was to their right, slightly hidden by a grove of old, regal-looking trees.

The road came to a stop at these trees, just as Anthony had stated. They'd now have to walk about a quarter of a mile through the trees and to a muddy bank.

"Look at this," Palmer said as they got out. He was pointing to a patch of ground slightly to his left. The grass out here was up to their calves, so the recent tire marks coming through it were plain to see. They then both looked over toward the trees and though the path of where someone had recently walked wasn't quite as clear, it was most definitely there.

They followed the slight indentations in the grass and passed into the tree line. For the second time that day, they walked across muddy ground that was mostly covered with damp, dead foliage.

When they came out of the trees, the ground swept hard to the right, creating a crescent-shaped bank that was surprisingly dry. They walked along it for several yards before Camille spotted patrol footprints in the sand; they were both coming and going, showing that someone had been through here quite a bit as of late.

The sandy bank continued arcing to the right and as they came around a thin grove of weeds and cluttered vines, the swamplands seemed to open up in front of them, giving them a peek of what was out in the deeper regions of the forest.

The water that sat to their left was clear at the edge along the bank but it became dark almost right away. Countless small trees sprouted out of the water and more varieties of grass and weeds than Camille could count did the same.

Roughly thirty yards away from the bank, anchored to a massive tree that looked as if it were ancient, was a worn-down houseboat. To call it a houseboat was a stretch, though; it looked more like a large pontoon boat that someone had slapped a few rooms on.

Camille scanned the bank and saw an old aluminum fishing boat tied up to a fallen log not too far away. She walked over to it and peered inside. There were few old cake wrappers inside, as well as what looked to be an old cutting board with dried fish guts on it.

"Let's say all of this is indeed Kyle Harlan's," Camille said. "I'd say it's a safe bet he's not home."

"And it's starting to get dark," Palmer said. "You think he's out looking for another victim?"

"I do."

And as she said this, she recalled Anthony's story. Anthony had been the prized son, in a way, and Kyle seemed to always come in second place. Kyle was the kid that was bullied and maybe even ignored by his older brother and his father. Even when he'd been treed by that gator, neither of them had really….

"And I think I might even know who it is," she said.

"Care to share?" Palmer said.

"I think it's Reed Harlan."

"The father?"

Without so much as discussing it, Camille untied the aluminum boat and stepped on. Palmer followed, careful to keep his balance as the boat shook and swayed in the dark water.

"Think about it. Kyle wasn't in those records for reported gator attacks. And he also wasn't ever invited out to go on those trips with his father and brother. And finally, think of the way Anthony spoke about him."

Camille used the single paddle in the boat to push them out to the houseboat. The swamp stank of sour earth and rotting things. Knowing there were gators out here made it an even more precarious trip to the houseboat.

"You think he feels jilted by his father," Palmer said. "You think he maybe even blames his father for his attack."

"Maybe. It's just guesswork right now, but I think...yeah, I think it feels right."

She brought the boat alongside the edge of the houseboat. It was mildewed and bleached by God only knew how many years of sunlight. When they stepped on the back of the houseboat, it creaked under their feet.

Quickly, with a suspect and a potential next victim in mind (and a sun that was quickly retreating behind the horizon), they started to search the place over even though there was clearly no one on board.

The floor inside had been white at one point, but was now chipped and gray as it had settled over the years. There were old newspapers and magazines scattered here and there. Old, empty food cans and discarded plastic cutlery. On a paper plate, Camille noted what looked to be the small, brittle bones of an animal. Maybe a squirrel. More like a frog, though. A short, narrow staircase in the back of the boat led up to the second-floor deck. This took them into a kitchen area. It held a single counter littered with pots and pans, a small sink with a broken pipe, and a rusted old refrigerator that clearly hadn't been used in years.

"All this little visit has done is creep me right the hell out," Palmer said.

"Same," Camille agreed. "Let's head back out. As soon as we get cell signal, I think we need to call Humphrey, get an APB out on Kyle and Reed Harlan."

"Maybe if Anthony thinks his father is in trouble, he'll finally tell us where he is?"

"Doubtful. I'm pretty sure he's not telling us where his father is because his father is likely out doing the very thing he'd gotten in trouble for."

"Trapping and hunting alligators?"

"Yes...and with an estranged son who is using them to help kill people."

With that final thought spoken, they stepped back out onto the rickety aluminum boat and made their way back across the swampy water, which was growing blacker as dusk finally settled down across the county.

***

"Humphrey, I need you to keep this under wraps, but we're fairly certain Reed Harlan is in danger. Do what you can to get Anthony to fess up to where he is."

There was a brief silence on the other end of the line. Camille wondered if the call had broken up. She and Palmer were still on the dirt roads out by the swamp, Palmer guiding the truck down the bumpy, nasty roads as fast as he could without killing them.

"Did you catch that, Humphrey?"

"Yeah, I got it. What makes you think—"

"We also need eyes out on the younger Harlan brother, Kyle."

There was a pause again, which Humphrey finally ended with "Roger on that, too."

"We're about twenty minutes out," Camille said. "While I've got you on here, can you try to locate a phone number for Reed Harlan?"

"Yeah, I can do that. Anything else?"

"Not right now. But if it's all the same to you, I'd like to keep you on the line as you try to sort all of this out."

There was some clicking and jostling from Humphrey's end as he moved through the station. "I'm about to head in to speak with Anthony. Want me to put you on speaker? We might get everything you need out of one conversation with him."

"Good idea. Yeah, do that."

Palmer swerved to miss a bump but didn't quite avoid it. The right side of the truck dropped down a bit, the shocks squealing. As he righted it, Camille could hear the door to the interrogation room at the Hen Creek police station opening up.

She heard Humphrey speaking, listening to a conversation that sounded like it was taking place on the other side of the world.

"Anthony, I've got Agent Grace on the line. I think you might want to speak with her."

"What for?"

"Just speak to her, Harlan. We've about had it with your smart mouth." There was a final shuffling sound and then Humphrey said: "Go ahead, Agent Grace."

"Anthony, we need to know where your father is. We believe he might be in danger."

"Make up your mind, would you?" Anthony snapped. "One minute you're going after my dad, then Kyle, now you're back to my dad again. I mean, what do you—"

"Those names I gave you earlier?" Camille said. "Earl Stewart, Wendy Pullman, Gary Anderson. They're all dead, Anthony. They were murdered by someone who is using them as a strange sort of bait for alligators. All three of them. And we know for sure that two of them had run-ins with your brother that weren't great, right?"

The silence from the other end sounded heavy. It lasted about five seconds before Anthony's voice filled her ear. On the other side of the truck windshield, Palmer had brought them to the end of the dirt routes and back to the unmarked blacktop. The headlights shone out, glowing through the dust the truck had kicked up.

"Kyle...he wouldn't do that. He just wouldn't do it. He...shit. Are you serious about all of this?"

"I'm afraid so, Anthony. And even if there was only a small chance we're right on this, wouldn't you want us to stop it from happening?"

Anthony screamed a loud curse from the other end of the line.

"Anthony?..."

"You have to go back to his house, to dad's house," Anthony said. Camille heard the genuine worry in his voice, which helped her to actually believe he was helping. "Just a little ways past his driveway, there's a dirt road. It goes about a mile and a half straight back. When the roads ends, you have to get out and walk, but not far. There's a place there, a piece of swamp he always called The Pit. That’s where he'll be. And that's *if* he's still out there. It's getting too dark outside to do much of anything. I'd say you have maybe another half an hour."

Which, Camille thought, *means Kyle only has another half an hour, too. We might already be too late.*

"Got it," she said, and ended the call.

"Where we headed?" Palmer asked, the truck still parked at the junction of the dirt road and the blacktop.

"Back toward Reed's house. And hurry!"

CHAPTER TWENTY NINE

Camille's hands were clutching the dashboard, ready to spring out as soon as the truck came to a stop. They'd just passed by Reed Harlan's driveway and within just a few seconds, the small track that Anthony had mentioned could be seen on the right, just up ahead. Palmer took the turn with shocking speed and impact, the station's truck taking even more abuse as the body slammed up and down, the shocks working overtime.

The little road was very thin, with weeds growing in the center between the tire tracks. The end of the road appeared sooner than she expected, revealing a small strip of land that was completely overrun with tall weeds and meager, yet sickly-looking trees growing in the thick of it all.

As Palmer brought the truck to a stop, the headlights swept through the tall grasses lining the track, the tall weeds swishing back and forth to the rhythm of the truck. The early night ahead presented a milky dark that the headlights just barely penetrated.

When Camille got out of the truck, she instantly drew her Glock. Everything within her felt that this was the moment, that this was the place. She could feel it like a small electrical charge in her nerves. Even the night itself seemed to push her on, ushering her with urgency.

Palmer left the headlights on when he got out, falling directly in behind Camille. They made their way through the tall grass, some of it coming up as high as Camille's breasts. She could hear all manner of night creatures, coming out to greet the darkness. Crickets, frogs, something howling off in the distance.

And then, in the midst of it all, a scream tore through the night. It was followed almost immediately by a faint splashing noise.

It was more than enough for Camille to spring into action. She shifted from a steady march to an all-out run. She kept her Glock held down by her side, not sure what to expect: maybe Kyle Harlan trying to kill his father, maybe an alligator, maybe *anything*. In the midst of these darkening woods, she supposed anything was possible.

The swamp came into view, right along a shallow bank that the weeds followed down into the dark water, getting drowned out. The very faint glow of the headlights behind them barely illuminated anything. All Camille could see was the dark water and, about fifteen yards away, a man in the water, struggling to his feet.

She then heard Palmer behind her. "Shit..."

He strayed to the right, getting into a crouching position. "Kyle Harlan, you need to drop your weapon right now!"

Camille looked to the right, to where the bank rose up and seemed to reach into the forest. It was all nothing more than a blurry lens of shadows and dark shapes. But among all of that, she did see someone on the bank, making a run for it into the trees.

As Palmer took off after the figure—a figure she assumed was indeed Kyle Harlan—Camille did her best to get a clean shot on him. But it was just too damned dark and the trees were so tightly woven together that any sort of shot was impossible.

"I'll get him," Palmer said as he started asking forward. "You check on the victim."

She would have much rather it been the other way around, but she didn't see the point in arguing about it. Besides, there was no time.

She also realized that there was no way she could get to the victim without stepping out into the water. It was no big deal, she figured; he was out there, fifteen yards away, and the water seemed to only be up to his knees.

"Mr. Harlan?" she asked. "Reed Harlan?"

"Yeah..." he gasped.

"Are you injured?"

"He stabbed me. Right in the stomach...stabbed me."

"Hold on," she said. And then, grimacing, she stepped out into the water. The worst part of it was the feeling of the muck giving way under her feet.

That, and not being able to see much of anything around her or, more specifically, beneath the black water.

As she took two more steps forward, her eyes finally adjusted to the peculiar darkness. She could see the form of the man standing just ahead of her. He was holding onto a tree limb, hunched over.

"Mr. Harlan, I'm coming. You just stay right there, okay? Let's get you out of here."

"I'm fine," he said, though the weak waver in his voice indicated otherwise. "Get back on the bank. There are gators out here. I think...I think he was trying to feed me to them."

"My partner is going to get him, Mr. Harlan. And I'm already out here, so I'm—"

As if summoned by the mention of gators, the water came alive around her. It exploded in a splash of mud, the sound of it slamming into the reeds and all around Camille's body. She felt something large and hard strike her leg as it rushed past, half-in and half-out of the water.

She'd been knocked slightly off balance, but caught herself before she fell down completely. The water splashed around her, but her shoes kept her feet from being sucked down into the mud as she scanned the area.

She saw the gator to her left, circling back around her. She raised her gun, trying to get a clear shot. She had no idea how a Glock round would work on a gator but she figured she was going to find out soon enough.

The gator surged forward and in the darkness, she saw the teeth and the sick pink of its tongue. It slammed into her and this time there was no hope of keeping her feet. Camille went sprawling down into the water, into the mud. She felt the weight of the creature on top of her, fighting and scrambling for purchase. For a moment, it almost felt as if it were trying to embrace her and in that same flash of time, she could also smell its breath.

She grimaced as she did her best to crawl away from it, but it had her in its clutches. And before she could figure out how to fight against it, she felt herself being pulled back down into the water. Not only into it, but *beneath* it.

Filthy swamp water filled her mouth and nostrils. She gagged, which, being underwater, made it worse. In a panic, she lifted her Glock up…only to find that her hand was empty. She'd dropped it in the attack.

She thought back to when she'd saved Palmer, but given her current situation, she wasn't going to be able to punch it in its snout. In fact, if she didn't figure out a way to get her head above water, she was going to drown.

In a stroke of blind luck, the gator twisted in its attack and her face broke the surface. She was on her hands and knees, the gator pushing down against her. Its weight was immense and she felt herself being crushed. At the same time, the gator swiveled around, lessening the weight a bit.

Positioned at her right side, it opened its jaws. It was coming for her right side, wanting the meat along her ribs.

In a flash of what was both desperation and sudden enlightenment, Camille pivoted and presented herself to the gator from the front. It did not stop, but instead its jaws were now coming for her head.

And the moment it was there, its killer teeth less than a foot away from her face, Camille drew her hand back and, with a cry of expected pain, delivered a hard right-handed jab directly into its mouth.

Her arm went all the way in, past the elbow. She felt its tongue, then its throat. She also felt its teeth grazing her shoulder through her shirt. She felt skin tearing, but she also felt the clenching of its throat as she gagged it with her arm. She had no idea where she'd heard this trick (likely in the same place she's learned about popping it in the snout) but it seemed to be working.

The gator made a deep gagging noise, as if it were about to throw up. It then pushed away furiously, churning up dark water as it made a retreat.

Camille fell back into the water and when she did, her elbow struck something hard...something hard and familiar.

Her gun.

She reached down into the water, hoping it wasn't too waterlogged to fire. She pulled it up, took an uncertain shooter's stance in the mud, with her right shoulder on fire. She waited for the gator to come circling back and when it did, she fired at its head.

Gratefully, the Glock fired. She did not see it hit the gator, but she fired again, this time directly at its eye.

That did the trick. The gator rolled hard to the left and made its way deeper into the swamp.

"Christ, lady!" Reed Harlan said. "Are you crazy?"

"The verdict is out," Camille said as she got to her feet. She felt slightly sick, her nerves on fire from the realization of what she'd just done. If she'd been just half a second off in the thing of it all, she'd be missing an arm right now.

She made her way over to Harlan and saw that he was bleeding profusely from the stomach. She wasn't able to help him much; she had to use her left arm because her right shoulder was in horrendous pain and she could feel blood trickling down her arm. She was quite scared to take a look at it, to see what sort of damage had been done.

"Grace!"

The cry came out of the woods, Palmer's voice. He sounded like he was in pain and worried about something.

"Yeah, I'm good," she called back. "I'm here."

She made it to the bank with Reed Harlan just in time to see Palmer come out of the trees. He was pushing a stumbling Kyle Harlan with him, giving the young man a final shove that sent him down to the ground. He was cuffed and had a good amount of blood spilling from his mouth.

"Bastard cut me," Palmer said. His left arm was held close to his chest. Even in the darkness, Camille could see the gash on the underside of his forearm. It looked to be dumping blood out onto the bank.

"I'll make a call to Humphrey," she said.

"You good?" Palmer asked. "I hear shots."

"I'm f—"

"This crazy bitch stuck her arm down a gator's throat," Reed Harlan said, still in shock.

Palmer's laughter was both eerie but also fitting, Camille thought. "Of course she did," he said.

And then he stumbled backwards, fell against an old cypress, and continued to laugh.

It was just the distraction Kyle Harlan needed. He got to his feet and started to run. He ran back toward where Palmer had parked, where the faint glow of headlights could be seen.

Camille went for her gun again but moving so quickly, she grew slightly dizzy from the motion and the darkness. Somewhere ahead of her, she heard Kyle fall. Running, after all, wasn't as easy as people often thought it was while handcuffed.

There was the smacking noise of him hitting the ground and then the splashing noise of his rebound into the water.

"You're going to regret making me come back down into the water," Camille said. Hissing at the pain in her right shoulder, she took a single step forward.

The large shape of the gator came out of the water.

It came just barely up on the muddy shore, its jaws snapping down on Kyle's legs. The gator then gave a vicious pull backwards, retreating back into the water. Kyle screamed out but was unable to attempt to save himself with his arms cuffed behind his back. The scream was soon distorted by the swamp water, making a terrifying gurgling noise.

"Kyle!" Reed screamed. He ran forward but the wound to his stomach prevented him for moving very far. He screamed out in pain and anguish all at once, nearly falling to the ground.

"Jesus," Camille said. She rushed forward, Glock in hand.

But the gator was gone. She could barely see its shape underwater as it pulled its dinner away. She waded out into the water a bit, hoping for a better shot, but it was just too dark. Firing on a good guess would only mean there was also a good chance she'd hit Kyle.

In other words, there was nothing she could do.

Trembling, she holstered her Glock and pulled out her phone. She called Humphrey down at the station as the woods of Hen Creek were filled with Reed Harlan's screams of pain and loss.

CHAPTER THIRTY

Aside from the killer getting hauled off by an alligator, Camille considered the case a sweeping success. She'd come face to face with two alligators in the course of two days and had somehow only come away with twelve stitches in her shoulder.

This was why, at 11:40 on the night they'd rescued Reed Harlan, she was able to walk into Palmer's hospital room under her own power, of her own accord.

She found Palmer sitting up in bed, watching something on the History Channel on the mounted TV. He shrugged at her and showed her his left arm. It was wrapped tightly in a bandage from elbow to wrist.

"Yeah, I heard they wanted to keep you a bit longer," Camille said. "How bad was it?"

"I lost a good amount of blood," he said. "Took thirty-two stitches to close it up. He got me pretty good. I take it you're good to go?"

"Yeah. I'm going to head to call McCutcheon to give her an update. Then I'm going to get some sleep and see what I can do to help locate Kyle Harlan's body."

"Have you heard anything about Reed's condition?"

"He's in surgery right now," Camille said. "Based on what the doctors told me, he should come out of it fine. The stab was deep, but didn't seem to puncture anything."

"And you...you're good?" Palmer asked. "I mean, I know the wound is closed up and all, but you literally fought off two alligators in the last few days. That's got to screw a person up pretty good, right?"

She grinned and said, "Maybe. Probably, even. If we end up working together more in the future, maybe you can point out some of the deep, psychological traumas for me."

"Gladly. It was...well, it was interesting working with you again."

"Likewise. I'll check in with you tomorrow. Take it easy, Palmer."

She closed the door as she left and walked down the quiet hallway. A few nurses were scattered here and there but it had the silence and calm of a midnight-hour hospital wing.

She went to the elevator, took it down, and headed out to the parking lot. As she walked through the doors, angling over to the lot where Humphrey and Bradford had worked in tandem to make sure she had a car waiting for her, a slight motion to the right caught her eye. And then, her name came from the same direction.

"Agent Grace?"

She turned and saw a man standing up from a bench off to the side of the hospital entrance. It was Zack Hayes, the part-time zoologist she'd met with the day before.

"Zack? Hey. How are you?"

"I'm good. Better than you from what I hear."

"Are you visiting someone?" she asked.

"Um, technically, yes. I was here to visit you. But the folks at the front desk wouldn't give me the information. Apparently, it's hard to get the room information for an FBI agent that has just wrapped a case."

"How did you know I'd be here?"

He signed and shoved his hands into his pockets. "It's embarrassing. But I couldn't get the idea of a murder case involving alligators out of my mind. So I downloaded this police scanner app. I've sort of been following the case as well as I could since last night. I heard that there were two federal agents being rushed to the hospital from a location out by the swamps. And then when I got here, I asked about an Agent Camille Grace and the stubborn lady at the desk all but confirmed that you *were* here."

"Oh. well, I appreciate the gesture, but I'm actually fine. Just a few stitches."

"Gator bite?"

She chuckled. "Yeah, sort of."

"Can I ask how much longer you'll be in town?"

She considered it, not wanting to give out any details about why she may stay in the Hen Creek area. The fact that Kyle's body still needed to be found complicated things.

"At least another day or so."

"I see. Well, I may as well take the chance, then."

"What chance?" she asked.

"I'd like to take you out to dinner." He smiled nervously and added: "I wasn't *only* following the case on the app because of the gators."

"You know," she said, returning his smile. "So long as I don't end up in front of another gator tomorrow, dinner would be nice."

"Awesome...wait. In front of *another* gator? What on earth happened today?"

She gave him the best flirtatious smile she could manage given how tired she was and said: "Maybe we leave that for dinner conversation."

***

Her father seemed glad to see her. The tension and awkwardness of their first visit was no longer there. In fact, when she told him about the unique case she'd just finished up, he'd listened with rapt attention. He even asked to see her stitches, if she didn't find it too weird.

She *did* find it weird, but she showed him anyway. It was the most interest he'd ever showed in her. And grown-up or not, she craved his attention. She'd tried to deny it for her entire life, but there was the truth of it, plain and simple.

As evening settled in, Carl Grace insisted on grilling burgers. So they sat on his rickety back porch in plastic chairs while he cooked on his small charcoal grill. In the awkward silence, Camille let the haze of the last few days settle in.

In the end, she stayed in Hen Creek for two more days. Kyle Harlan's body was found at seven in the morning the following day, but she was asked to stay behind to help with a deep dive into whether or not there might potentially be more victims that had simply not yet been found.

When there was no evidence of more victims after thirty-six hours, she left Hen Creek behind. Before leaving, she nearly had dinner with Zack Hayes but ended up only calling, in order to postpone it. She had a feeling that Hayes was the persistent type and figured that if he was really interested, he'd call again.

After leaving Hen Creek, she did not head directly back to New Orleans. Instead, she drove a good distance out of her way to make a stop in Upping.

"You think this might work?" he asked her out of nowhere.

Swatting at a fly as they started to gather around the grill, Camille was pretty sure she knew what he meant but she wanted to be absolutely sure.

"Do I think *what* will work?"

"This," he said. "Me and you."

"I don't know. If I say it could, would you finally go see a specialist about your cancer?"

His shoulders sagged at the mention of it. She knew that even if they did continue to try to work on their relationship, his pancreatic cancer would be in the background, wailing like a ghost. Then again, if he kept avoiding treatment, this little relationship they were trying to salvage would be a very brief one.

"I don't know. It's a lot of trouble, Camille. A lot of money."

"I can help pay it."

"I'm not going to borrow money from my own child."

"And why not?"

Carl flipped the burgers one at a time, big, chunky ones that were starting to smell amazing over the coals.

"You sound just like Deanna, you know?" he said.

"I take that as a compliment."

"You should. You know she thinks the world of you, right?"

Camille said nothing to this. She thought she might go visit Deanna after burgers with her father. Maybe they could drink some wine and talk about completely nonsensical things.

"She thought a lot of Nanette, too. When Nanette visited her all those years ago, Deanna was on cloud nine for weeks."

The comment almost went unnoticed. But Camille grabbed hold of it and studied it, not liking the implications.

"Visited? When?"

Carl Grace's face went pale as he realized he'd misspoken. He looked away from her and muttered a curse under his breath.

"When, Dad? What...what aren't you telling me?"

"It was about eleven years ago. Maybe twelve. She just showed up and stopped by Deanna's. Didn't bother coming to see me, of course, but..."

"Twelve years ago? Dad...she disappeared *fifteen* years ago."

He only nodded. And it was all he needed to say.

"Is she...Jesus, Dad. Do you *know* she's alive?"

When he looked back to her, there were tears in his eyes. "Well, she was twelve years ago. Neither me or Deanna have seen her since."

"Why didn't you tell me? Why didn't Deanna tell me?"

"Because we both knew how much you loved her. If we gave you that hope and Nanette never stuck around...we didn't want to put you through that."

Camille wanted to cry. She wanted to scream. In the end, she did neither.

In the end, she simply said "Bye, Dad."

As she walked down the back porch steps, Carl called out to her. "We were just thinking about your best interests. And hell...I don't even know where she is now. Or if she's even still alive."

Each word was like a nail into her heart and by the time Camille returned to the front yard, she was weeping. When she got into her car, she wasn't all that surprised to find that her father hadn't bothered chasing her down to explain.

Backing out of his driveway, she couldn't help but think that she'd been right all along. She'd been better off to leave him in the past—to leave her entire miserable family in the past.

With tears still in her eyes and the hope of finding her sister now more realistic than ever, Camille sped away from the rural scar of her past and toward the city where her future was still waiting.

Her sister could be out there somewhere. And starting now, Camille was done waiting.

She'd find Nannette and, with her, maybe some more answers about a past that continued to haunt her.

NOW AVAILABLE!

NOT WELL
(A Camille Grace FBI Suspense Thriller—Book 3)

In this new series by #1 bestselling—and critically-acclaimed—mystery and suspense author Kate Bold, Camille Grace, a rising star in the FBI's BAU unit, is dispatched to the one place she vowed to never return: the deep South. When bodies turn up on steamboats on the Mississippi River, Camille realizes she is up against a diabolical serial killer—one who will not stop until she finds him.

"Phenomenal debut with a huge creep factor… So many twists and turns, you'll have no idea who the next victim will be. If you love a thriller that will keep you awake well into the night, this book is for you."
—Reader review for *Let Me Go*

Camille must come to terms with her partner, and with her own local roots, as she plunges headlong into the investigation. It will require every ounce of attention she has to enter this killer's mind and crack the code.

But a new lead into her own sister's disappearance may just upend everything.

A riveting psychological crime thriller full of mystery and suspense, the CAMILLE GRACE mystery series will make you fall in love with a brilliant new female protagonist. Packed with twists and turns, her story will keep you flipping pages late into the night.

The series begins with NOT ME (book #1), and future books in the series will soon be available.

"This is an excellent book… When you start reading, be sure you don't have to wake up early!"
—Reader review for The Killing Game

"I really enjoyed this book… It draws you in right away and keeps you turning the pages right up to the end. I am really anticipating the next book."
—Reader review for Let Me Go

"WOW what a great read! Talk about a diabolical killer! Really enjoyed this book. Looking forward to reading others by this author as well."
—Reader review for The Killing Game

"Excellent start to a new series… Get this book and read it, you will love it!"
—Reader review for Let Me Go

"Captivating and riveting serial murder with a twist of the macabre… Very well done."
—Reader review for The Killing Game

"Good read with good plot, plenty of action, and great character development. A thriller that will keep you awake into the night."
—Reader review for Let Me Go

Kate Bold

Bestselling author Kate Bold is author of the ALEXA CHASE SUSPENSE THRILLER series, comprising six books (and counting); the ASHLEY HOPE SUSPENSE THRILLER series, comprising six books (and counting); the CAMILLE GRACE FBI SUSPENSE THRILLER series, comprising five books (and counting); and the HARLEY COLE FBI SUSPENSE THRILLER series, comprising three books (and counting).

An avid reader and lifelong fan of the mystery and thriller genres, Kate loves to hear from you, so please feel free to visit www.kateboldauthor.com to learn more and stay in touch.

BOOKS BY KATE BOLD

ALEXA CHASE SUSPENSE THRILLER
THE KILLING GAME (Book #1)
THE KILLING TIDE (Book #2)
THE KILLING HOUR (Book #3)
THE KILLING POINT (Book #4)
THE KILLING FOG (Book #5)
THE KILLING PLACE (Book #6)

ASHLEY HOPE SUSPENSE THRILLER
LET ME GO (Book #1)
LET ME OUT (Book #2)
LET ME LIVE (Book #3)
LET ME BREATHE (Book #4)
LET ME FORGET (Book #5)
LET ME ESCAPE (Book #6)

CAMILLE GRACE FBI SUSPENSE THRILLER
NOT ME (Book #1)
NOT NOW (Book #2)
NOT WELL (Book #3)
NOT HER (Book #4)
NOT NORMAL (Book #5)

HARLEY COLE FBI SUSPENSE THRILLER
NOWHERE SAFE (Book #1)
NOWHERE LEFT (Book #2)
NOWHERE TO RUN (Book #3)

www.ingramcontent.com/pod-product-compliance
Lightning Source LLC
Chambersburg PA
CBHW030613310726
48979CB00003B/699

9781094394831